D0803850

What the press says about Harlequin Romances...

"...clean, wholesome fiction...always with an upbeat, happy ending."
— *San Francisco Chronicle*

"...a work of art."
— *The Globe & Mail*, Toronto

"Nothing quite like it has happened since *Gone With the Wind...,*"
— *Los Angeles Times*

"...among the top ten..."
— *International Herald-Tribune*, Paris

"Women have come to trust these clean, easy-to-read love stories about contemporary people, set in exciting foreign places."
— *Best Sellers*, New York

OTHER
Harlequin Romances
by CHARLOTTE LAMB

Florentine Spring

by

CHARLOTTE LAMB

Harlequin Books

TORONTO • LONDON • NEW YORK • AMSTERDAM • SYDNEY

Original hardcover edition published in 1977
by Mills & Boon Limited

ISBN 0-373-02103-8

Harlequin edition published September 1977

Printed in U.S.A

CHAPTER ONE

SHE liked to arrive early whenever she was cooking at a new place. Kitchens, like people, varied so enormously. She had to feel her way into the layout of the room, work out a smooth routine, a pattern of movement from oven to work-top and back to the sink. She had always found that half an hour spent in familiarising herself with these details paid off handsomely during the actual cooking.

Today she found herself in a small, cramped room at the end of a narrow corridor. The flat itself seemed spacious and elegant, judging by what she had seen as the hostess whisked her past the several rooms, yet the most important room had been ludicrously ill-designed. Cupboards were tiny and ill-lit. The refrigerator was squashed into a corner and only just held a handful of items. The worktops were at the wrong height, so that she had to stoop in order to see what she was doing.

'Ghastly, isn't it?' The hostess smiled apologetically. She was more or less the same age as Nicola, but exceedingly well dressed. Her sleek dark hair was swathed on top of her head, exposing a slim, tanned throat and shoulders. She had a faintly Latin appearance, despite her obviously English accent, and the black lace mantilla she wore around her shoulders deepened the impression.

Nicola returned the smile smoothingly. 'I'll manage, don't worry. I've cooked in worse kitchens than this one!'

Mrs Christiansen grimaced. 'I didn't think there were any! I'm so grateful to see you—you can't imagine! I only had my baby six weeks ago and I'm still desperately trying to cope with the new situation. My husband has these important dinner parties from time to time. They're part of his job, you know. He's very understanding, but I know he feels I should be able to manage the baby and arrange everything for his party, too.'

'Men expect us to wave a magic wand,' agreed Nicola, smiling. 'I know what they're like!'

'So that is why I rang your agency! Your suggestion for a menu was fantastic, by the way. I adore *boeuf en croute*. Are you sure you can manage it in this kitchen?'

Nicola grinned. 'Oh, the *boeuf en croute* is already cooked. I did that in my own oven at home and brought it with me—I shall re-heat it in time to serve it. Don't worry, it will taste fine. I have it wrapped in foil.' She began to unpack her basket, hoping that Mrs Christiansen would take the hint and leave her to get on with her tasks.

But the other girl was clearly bored and lonely. She leaned against the door, watching Nicola curiously.

'Carl is asleep, and I only have to change. Can I do anything to help?'

Nicola shook her head. 'No, thank you, I can manage. We have certain tricks of the trade, you know—corner-cutting! The soup is in this screw-top flask, you see, already prepared. Here is the paté, and here are the fresh sardines. I have to cook the vegetables—all freshly bought, and they will taste delicious, I assure you. Some of them are prepared for cooking, too. It all saves times.'

Mrs Christiansen laughed. 'You have it worked out to the last item, don't you? I wish I could be as efficient. I'm a hopeless housewife. I can't cook. I panic if the baby sneezes. And I hate ironing.'

Nicola hesitated, then glanced at her. 'You don't have any help in the flat?'

The other girl flushed. 'Yes, I have a daily help. But I would like to be able to do it myself.' She paused, biting her lip. 'I married straight from school. My husband has been moved three times during our married life—we have lived in Rio, in Milan and here in London. It is much easier to get domestic help abroad than it is here in England.'

'So I've heard,' said Nicola crisply. She was working while she talked, her slim hands deft and efficient, her clear-skinned face bearing just the faintest flush. The silky dark hair was worn casually tied at the nape of the neck by a ribbon, to keep it out of her way while she worked. 'How did you like Italy?'

'Italy?' The other girl laughed involuntarily. 'Why,

I ...' She broke off as the door bell pinged. 'Oh, sorry —I must answer that!'

Nicola sighed with relief as the door shut behind her. At last she could get on with her work without feeling bound to talk. She worked much better when she could concentrate.

The meal was almost ready for serving when the hostess finally returned to the kitchen. Nicola was standing by the oven, surveying the various pots with a thoughtful eye, doing a last-minute check on everything.

'How is it going?' Mrs Christiansen stood in the doorway, her coral evening dress giving a delightful new colour to her skin. She had an excited sparkle in her dark eyes and a curve to her lips.

'I'm ready when you are,' Nicola smiled. She had slipped a frilly white apron over her neat black dress, transforming herself into a waitress.

The other girl sighed. 'That's wonderful! My husband will be so pleased! Our last dinner party was a complete fiasco—it started an hour late and was uneatable—the food, I mean!' She looked eagerly at the simmering soup. 'I checked the dining-room just now. It looks marvellous. I really do admire your cool efficiency —by the way, what is your name? Please, call me Carla.'

'I'm Nicola.' She smiled warmly, feeling a sudden liking for the other girl. This eager, pleasant manner was such a change from the way in which she was often treated by the people who hired her services. Some people seemed to think that she was a sort of robot, a machine without feeling or intelligence, who would not have the sensitivity to know when she was being snubbed or insulted. 'Shall I serve now, then?'

'Please! I'll go and ask the guests to move through into the dining-room. Good luck!' And Carla vanished with a last cheerful smile.

There were six guests seated in the charming dining-room when Nicola entered, pushing her wheeled trolley before her. The host sat at the furthest end of the table, facing her as she entered. She had a brief impression of fair hair, beard and bronzed face above the usual evening clothes. The others sat, three to a side, male and female alternately. The tall, twisty red candles gave a gentle glow to their faces. The mellow light glinted on silver and glass, chequered the mixed carnations in the centre of the table, making the white ones dark.

The conversation died briefly, then began again, rather too consciously.

Nicola began serving the soup, then went round the table again with sardines to those who had refused soup. No one wanted the paté. She withdrew quietly with her trolley and re-loaded it with the main course, with an alternative of salad on the lower deck. Guests sometimes ruined these parties by being difficult over some dishes and she usually found it useful to have a salad available, with egg mayonnaise or prawns in reserve.

Tonight everyone chose to have the beef, smoking

hot and tender in its envelope of pastry. The fresh, well-cooked vegetables were abundant; baby carrots, peas, new potatoes, all served in butter.

While she was serving a young woman with short, light hair she felt herself under observation, and shooting a glance across the table met the eyes of the man opposite.

He, like his host and hostess, had a beautiful deep tan, but he had the advantage of having a sallow skin to begin with, and dark hair which was sleeked down now but which had a springy, ruffled look at the back which, she suspected, was his usual look when he did not remember to brush his hair down firmly. The eyes which met hers were a clear, cool grey. They were assessing her impersonally from beneath well-shaped dark brows. Seeing the instinctive resentment which sprang into her own eyes, the stranger half-smiled, a curiously amused movement of the corners of his mouth.

Nicola glanced quickly away and went on with her task, but she had a vaguely uneasy feeling that she had seen him somewhere before.

When she had finished serving the beef, Carla Christiansen smiled at her. 'Thank you, Nicola!'

She smiled back, then, as she was backing her trolley out of the door, once more caught the grey-eyed stranger staring. His expression now was unreadable, but she again felt a flicker of uneasiness as the same sense of familiarity filled her.

Had she met him before? But where? At some other dinner party, perhaps? In the last year she had served at so many. It was impossible to recall all the faces of the guests, although her memory for faces and names was usually excellent.

Why did this one man fill her with a strange foreboding? She was not given to such fanciful feelings, normally.

When she returned with the cold dessert, a choice between a sherry trifle and fresh fruit salad and cream, she felt a pang of further alarm to hear some of the guests speaking in rapid Italian.

Of course, it was nonsense to let that disturb her. London was full of Italians. Sooner or later she had been bound to run into some. There was no reason why any of them should recognise her.

Nevertheless, it was with deep relief that she finally cleared the table and began the washing up. This task, too, she had well organised. Some of it had already been done, in the intervals between courses, by the simple expedient of soaking the dishes in hot water so that they were easy to wash.

She had almost finished when the kitchen door opened. She glanced round, expecting Mrs Christiansen.

It was the grey-eyed stranger.

'Good evening,' he said in perfect English. 'I hope I'm not intruding, but I wanted to have a word with you before you left.'

'I'm sorry,' Nicola said stiffly, 'I'm very busy. If the meal was not satisfactory . . . '

He cut her short with a gesture, his eyes narrowing

11

at her tone. 'The meal was superb. That is nothing to do with what I have to say. Correct me if I'm wrong, but ...'

A face appeared at his elbow and Mrs Christiansen interrupted him, her voice rising in astonishment.

'Domenico? What *are* you doing in the kitchen?' Then she gave an amused smile. 'Or am I being indiscreet?'

For a moment, the stranger seemed to hesitate, his face blank. Then he laughed. 'I was congratulating your cook on that amazing meal—remembering other meals I have eaten under your roof, my dear Carla!'

Now, as these two spoke to each other, Nicola could hear the faint echo of an Italian accent beneath their perfect English. It sounded most clearly when they spoke each other's names.

'Go back to the others, Nico! I have matters to discuss with Nicola now.' Carla shooed him casually, as a mother shoos a child, her face full of affection. He obeyed her, smiling, but turned before closing the door to look sharply at Nicola.

'I don't know how to thank you,' Carla said gratefully. 'You have made the evening a great success. My husband's business friends were impressed. I have no doubt I shall be bombarded with questions about you! Tell me, do you find this work rewarding? You like cooking?'

'I love it,' Nicola smiled.

'But do you work every evening?'

'Most evenings, yes.'

12

'Do you not find that a burden sometimes? Wouldn't you rather work during the day? At a hotel, for instance? Or a good London restaurant?'

'Most really good London restaurants and hotels prefer to engage men. Women, oddly enough, are at a disadvantage at that level of the catering trade. I like to work in private homes, to meet people. And working for the agency I can pick and choose my times of work. I can always ask for a week off without becoming too unpopular. Sometimes I don't work for days, then I work every night for several weeks. The money evens up in that way.'

'You are not married, of course?' Carla sighed.

Nicola's face was pale. 'No,' she said flatly.

Carla misread her tone. 'Oh, I'm sorry—am I being too impertinent? To be honest, I took a liking to you on sight, and my guests are more business acquaintances of my husband than friends of mine—apart from Nico, of course,' and again her face lit up as she said his name.

Nicola watched her curiously. She seemed strangely attached to the grey-eyed Domenico. Were they related? Or old friends?

Carla moved back to the door. 'I shall tell the agency how pleased I am when I pay them. Would it offend you if I gave you a tip?'

'It is very kind of you, but tips have to go into a common pool. Thank you for offering—please add it to your cheque when you pay.'

'It seems so impersonal,' Carla said wistfully. Im-

13

pulsively she unclasped a very pretty bracelet from her wrist and offered it to Nicola. 'It is only costume jewellery, of course. Please, keep it as a memento. We shall be leaving London quite soon, going back to Italy. It will suit you. The green stones bring out the colour of your eyes.'

Nicola was touched. 'How very kind! Thank you. I shall treasure it.'

She left early, half afraid that Domenico would come back once Carla had rejoined her guests, and hurried home. It was just striking eleven by the hall clock as she let herself into the flat she shared with her sister, Vanessa, and her school-friend, Bess Walsh.

Both of them were in bed. Vanessa was always in bed by ten-thirty. She was a fashion model, at present much sought after by photographers because her elegantly feline features somehow fitted the modern scene. Vanessa's life was ruled by laws more unalterable than those of the Medes and the Persians. Ruthlessly she forced herself to rise at seven. A leisurely bath was followed by a breakfast of orange juice and black coffee. Then she spent an hour getting dressed. She left for work punctually, worked long, arduous hours, and ate only as much as would preserve the breath of life, without adding an ounce of flesh to her slender body.

Tall, perfectly poised, with blonde hair curled in tight, abundant little ringlets, her blue eyes were fringed by long, false black lashes which deepened the blue to violet in some lights.

Bess was curved and small, with huge brown eyes,

rather like the centre of a pansy, and masses of soft, silky-brown hair to match. She was Nicola's oldest friend. They had been at school together from the age of five upwards, and had progressed side by side through high school and on to the same domestic science college later.

Only after they had both completed their education did they part for a while, but the parting had been brief, although, on Nicola's side, it had been deeply influential. Those six months apart from Bess had been the most eventful of her life. When she met Bess again she felt she was a different person, and she had been grateful for Bess's kindness and sympathy at that time.

Bess was not a sponge, soaking up tears, however, or a cushion on which to lean. She was sturdy, sensible, full of calm common sense, and immeasurably reassuring when one was unhappy.

She had decided to teach, on qualifying in domestic science, and she found it satisfying to show others how to do the things she did so well, herself.

She had been teaching at a local school for the last three years. Nicola depended on her, for support and help, but recently she had begun to wonder how much longer she would be able to do so. Bess had become increasingly friendly with one of the other teachers, a friendly, quiet man who taught mathematics. They were neither of them demonstrative people, but Nicola suspected that they were growing very close.

Even Vanessa, rarely observant where other people were concerned, had said the other day, 'Bess is beginning to smell of orange blossom. We shall have to find a new flatmate.'

Flatmates were easy to find, but where would Nicola find another reliable babysitter for Paul?

She tiptoed into the bedroom she shared with him. A faint light shone beside his cot. He lay, curled on his side, a pink hand against his cheek, lips apart, lashes thickly clustered on his curved cheek.

The dark hair, golden skin and fine features were all so poignantly familiar. She stood, looking down at him, sighing. He grew more like his father every day! Sometimes she wondered if she could bear it, and at other times she knew that he was healing scars inflicted by love and loss, gently burying bitter memories beneath fresh ones of joy and delight.

She could never bear to lose him! She turned, on an impulse, and went softly back to the shared sitting-room of the flat. She dialled a number, standing in the dark. It rang for a long time, but at last someone picked up the receiver, and a cross, sleepy voice asked, 'Yes, who is this?'

'Drew, it's Nicky.'

'Nicky? Good lord, girl, do you know what time it is? You know I go to bed early during the week!'

'I'm sorry, but it was urgent,' she said.

'Did something ghastly happen at your booking? Nicky, you weren't molested? I've always been afraid of something like that ...'

'No, Drew. It ...'

'You burnt the dinner? Did they blow their tops?

I'll defend you, my dear. Don't get excited ...'

'Drew, will you *listen*?'

He took a long breath, laughed. 'Sorry, *mea culpa*! Speak, I am all ears.'

'All tongue, you mean!'

'Darling, so beastly!'

'Drew, stop interrupting! Listen, if anyone asks for my name and address you won't give it to them, will you? No matter what they say?'

There was a little silence. She could picture him, his eyes narrowed in intelligent conjecture, his honey-coloured hair ruffled from sleep. Drew was far too shrewd for concealment to be possible.

'Darling,' he drawled at last, 'you know it's a house rule—Christian names only. No surnames or addresses. I've always stuck rigidly to it, haven't I?'

'Yes, I know,' she admitted. 'But ...'

'This time it's different?' His voice was thoughtful. 'How very interesting. Why, exactly? Who's on your trail? Thwarted lover? Jilted old flame?'

'Neither,' she said crisply. 'I think I'll take a few days off, Drew. Can you cancel any bookings you've taken for me?'

'I'll take a look in the book tomorrow. Call in early in the morning, will you? I'll pay you and confirm that you're free for a while.'

Nicola rang off and wearily went into the bathroom to wash and clean her teeth. It was almost midnight by the time she finally fell into bed.

She dreamt of Paolo, following him endlessly through

17

dark mazes of dreams, where his slim figure seemed always just out of reach, yet tantalisingly close. Once he turned to look back and smile at her, but his features dissolved in a sickeningly elusive fashion, and she found herself staring at the face of the grey-eyed stranger she had met earlier that night. She woke, sobbing in bitter disappointment, to hear Paul calling her.

'Mummy ... up! Up *now*, Mummy! Want up now ...'

It was just seven-thirty. She felt heavy-eyed and dull. She lifted Paul from his cot and took him through into the bathroom. Vanessa was just drifting out of it, leaving the room heavily scented and the windows steamy.

Vanessa kissed Paul, gave her sister a vague smile and vanished in the direction of the kitchen, her brief white towelling robe making her look like an elegant boy with long brown legs.

Bess had already prepared Paul's breakfast when Nicola carried him into the kitchen. His orange juice stood on the tray of his chair beside a boiled egg which was keeping warm beneath a vivid yellow egg-cosy in the shape of a felt chicken.

Paul silently set to, being an eager trencherman, and while he was busy with his egg Nicola sat down to nibble a slice of thin toast.

'An egg would do you good,' said Bess, eyeing her. 'You look wan this morning. Sickening for a cold?'

She shook her head. 'Bad night.'

'Paul's teeth?'

'No, just my own thoughts,' said Nicola.

'What's wrong?' Bess looked worried.

'Nothing, really. I think I need a break. I've done a lot of late work recently. I've asked Drew for some time off.'

Bess nodded. 'Good idea. Paul should be old enough for the nursery school soon—then you could get a part-time job during the daytime.'

When Nicola arrived at the agency office Drew greeted her with a broad grin.

'I've had two inquiries already, ducky—one from a man with a very deep voice. I choked him off, and he didn't protest too much. Soon afterwards I got a call from the woman who hired you last night. She wanted your address so that she could thank you personally, she said, but I refused. She tried to insist, but it did her no good, so she rang off, too. She wanted to book you again, she said, for tonight. I told her you were otherwise engaged for the next week.'

'Thank you, Drew. I'm very grateful.' Nicola was conscious that she was trembling, and she hoped that her voice was not too betraying.

Drew looked at her closely. 'Now, do tell—what is it all about, darling? The feller, I could understand. But why the female?'

'It's too complicated,' she said quickly.

He gave her a cheque and a duplicated statement. 'These are the jobs you've done. This is your share of the tips ...' He explained the various details briefly, and she thanked him as she put the cheque away.

The telephone rang just as she was leaving, and

Drew took her hand to detain her with a silent gesture.

He spoke in a tone which told her that this was a highly valued client. When he had put the telephone down, he grimaced at her. 'Sorry, ducky, that was the Countess of Navestock—she wants you to cook for her tonight—a very important dinner for two. She asked for you by name, so I could hardly refuse. She always praises you to the skies.'

'For two? But she always has her own maid for small meals. It's only for the big formal occasions that she calls us in, usually!'

'Her maid is off sick, apparently. Food poisoning, no doubt.' Drew laughed. 'Nicky dear, I'm sorry. I can't afford to offend her, though, especially as she always mentions us to her friends. I've had a dozen clients, at least, through her dropping our name. That sort of word of mouth advertising is worth gold.'

She sighed. 'I suppose so. All right, Drew, I'll do it. What menu, did she say?'

'She leaves it to you. Buy it and bring it with you. Expense no object.'

'Something really special?'

'I gathered so! Enjoy yourself for once—cook your favourite recipes.'

Nicola found the idea vaguely appealing. It would certainly make a change to cook a small meal really superbly.

She pushed Paul in his pushchair down to her favourite shops and bought various ingredients. Then she rang Bess at the school to ask if she would be able to babysit again that night. She had a rota of sitters for when Bess and Vanessa were both out, but it would need time to organise it.

Bess was free, and curious about the Countess. 'Is she entertaining a lover, perhaps?'

'She's seventy years old,' Nicola laughed.

'So what? There's no age limit, is there? It's time you found yourself another man, Nicky. You're stiffening at the mental joints.'

Nicola did not answer. Pain stabbed suddenly, making her dumb with anguish.

'Oh, Nicky, I'm sorry,' Bess said impulsively. 'I should have held my tongue, but I can't help feeling that you must put the past behind you one day, and the longer you put it off the harder it will be for you.'

'It's probably the correct attitude,' Nicola said angrily. 'I've no doubt I'm a psychological mess! But it's one thing to talk about it, another thing to do it.'

'Nicky, he's dead! He'll never come back!' Bess spoke gruffly, conscious of the bitterness she must be causing.

'I know he's dead!' Nicola's voice broke. 'I never forget it for an instant.'

'But you don't believe it—not believe it in an accepting way, Nicky. You're hanging on to him all the time, aren't you? You won't let him go.'

'Bess, you don't understand ...' Nicola swallowed hard, then said more calmly, 'I must go now. See you later.'

Paul was asleep when she left the flat that evening.

21

She found her way to the Countess's adorable little Chelsea house, which was only a stone's throw from their own flat, and rang the door bell.

When the door opened her heart missed a beat and turned over. The man who had opened the door was the grey-eyed stranger, Domenico.

Instinctively, without thinking, Nicola turned for flight. His hand shot out and caught her wrist. His fingers were long, cool and very strong.

'It isn't any good,' he said gently. 'I recognised you at once. I saw a photograph of you once. I was certain you were that girl with long dark hair and a face lit by a million candles ...' He had dropped into Italian, fluent and easy, knowing that she would comprehend him.

She tried to pretend, shaking her head. 'I'm sorry ... what did you say?'

But she knew it was hopeless, and so did he, his smile faintly sardonic.

'You and I are related, you see.' He shrugged. 'Paolo was my cousin! A second cousin only, but I knew him from birth upwards. He told me many things about you, Nicola. He was very much in love with you.'

Hot, blinding tears sprang to her eyes. She pulled at her hand to free it from his grip. 'Let me go! I want no part of your family. The Farenze family ignored my existence while Paolo was alive. They sent no one to his funeral. I only want to forget them now.' She kicked his ankle hard and fled, taking advantage of his momentary surprise. There was an alley running behind the houses and she ducked into it, hiding in the shadow of a crooked, ill-grown lime tree beside the crumbling wall. His footsteps came hastily towards the alley, paused as he glanced along it, then went hurriedly past up the road.

CHAPTER TWO

WHEN the sound of Domenico's footsteps had died away, Nicola walked slowly out of the alley, tears spilling down her cheeks. A cat in one of the hidden gardens gave a long, ear-splitting scream which made her jump. A car drove past, its headlights piercing the darkness, making her momentarily blind.

She jumped and gave a terrified gasp as a figure stepped out of the shadows and seized her arm firmly.

'You're going to have to speak to me sooner or later, Nicola. Why not get it over with?'

She sighed slowly, in resignation, and said icily, 'Very well, as you're so persistent, but I would prefer it if you would call me Miss Mayfield.'

'Why do you call yourself by your maiden name? Are you ashamed of Paolo's name?'

'I want nothing to do with his family—I prefer to forget that he was a Farenze.' She wanted to sound dignified, yet was uneasily afraid that she merely sounded ungracious.

'And so you have cut your husband out of your memory?' The deep voice was stern.

'Hardly that. I loved Paolo. His name was irrelevant

to that love.'

'A man is what his past has made him, and the Farenze family made Paolo,' said Domenico quietly.

'He cut himself free from them,' she cried indignantly. 'After he had come here to England, he felt finally emancipated from the shackles of your family history. For most of his life the family attempted to bind him. Only by escaping from Italy altogether could he find himself.'

'Is that what he told you?' asked Domenico thoughtfully, guiding her back to the Countess's house.

'Yes, Paolo told me the whole truth. We were very close.' Her voice quivered and she lifted her chin defiantly.

Domenico closed the front door and turned to face her in the soft light of the chandelier which hung above them. His grey eyes were speculative. 'I sometimes think it is a tragic error that the English do not go into strict mourning for the dead. This stiff upper lip of yours is not always a good idea. You are clearly still trapped in the web of grief. You speak of Paolo as though he were transparent as glass.'

'To me he was!'

He shook his head. 'No. He was an Italian, subtle and delicate, yet strong as the thread of the silkworm. Paolo certainly spoke the truth to you—the truth you wished to hear. But what of all the other truths, those truths you did not wish to hear? Are they not equally true?'

She looked at him without comprehension. 'What

are you talking about? Do you deny that your family wished to own Paolo, to force him to do their bidding? That after he had broken away, met me and we were married, they refused to write to him in acknowledgment of his news? That they never wrote to him again?'

Gravely he shrugged his broad shoulders, in a silent, Italianate gesture. After he had hesitated for a moment, he said, 'These are one picture of the facts. Yes, it is true that the family wished Paolo to obey. His father is an old man—he was fifty when Paolo was born. It is hard for the old to understand, to communicate with the young. Paolo was the younger of two sons. The elder was to inherit most of the estate. It is stupid to divide and thus to weaken. Paolo, his father desired, should marry one of his cousins, a wealthy heiress. Thus he, too, would be provided for, would be safe. But Paolo refused—worse, he left home. His father was angry, was heartbroken.'

'Heartbroken? Do you expect me to believe that? After what happened?'

'Please, wait. Judge when you know more. There is much you do not understand. Paolo wrote to say he had married. Whom, the family eagerly demanded, had he chosen—this Paolo who had refused a wealthy heiress? Can you imagine their feelings when they heard that he had chosen ... a cook? A servant?'

'Of all the snobbish ...!' Nicola choked with bitter humiliation. 'So that's why? I wasn't good enough for the Farenze family?'

26

'Paolo did not explain that that was why they were so angry?'

'He only said that they'd wanted him to marry for money, not love,' she said, her eyes flashing. 'Paolo told me the truth, as I said. He only left out the most wounding part of the truth. He didn't want me to know they had rejected me personally.'

He had been speaking in Italian. Now he reverted to English, and spoke more rapidly. 'His father might have forgiven him in time had he not been taken ill, himself, soon after your marriage. The shock caused a stroke. He did recover, slowly, but when your telegram arrived informing the family of Paolo's death, his father was still desperately ill. It was thought better to keep the news from him for the time being, but I was under the impression that someone wrote to you with the family sympathy. Surely wreaths were sent?'

'Nothing,' she said coldly. 'Paolo went to his grave with no mourners but myself and my family.'

'I do not understand that,' he said, frowning. 'There must have been a mistake. I was certain ...' He broke off, shrugging. 'Well, that must wait. There are other things to discuss. Paolo was not the only loss for his father. Three months ago Paolo's brother, Cesare, died of a tropical disease, while he was in Africa on a sales mission.'

'I'm sorry,' she said stiffly. 'He was married, wasn't he? Did he have children?'

'No, there were no children. His wife died in child-

27

birth a year ago. The child died, too. She was a delicate little creature, poor Luciana.'

'So the Farenze estate passes to ... who?' Nicola was pale and suddenly alarmed. Did he know, had he found out, about Paul? She had never considered the legal question before, knowing that Paolo had had nothing to leave his son. But now, with the Farenze estate possibly his inheritance, what should she do?

She wanted nothing to do with Paolo's family. She had deliberately omitted to inform them of Paul's birth. She had wanted no part of the Farenze family, and she had suspected that, if they knew she expected a child, they might attempt to interfere, even, perhaps, to try to make some legal claim for the child.

Now her doubts remained, but her fears were deeper. Paul was English, was hers. His father's family should have no part of him.

Domenico was speaking casually. 'There is no direct heir now. No doubt Lorenzo will decide when he makes his will—so far he has refused to make one.'

'But until he does? Who would succeed?'

'I fancy I am the nearest male heir,' Domenico shrugged.

She looked at him curiously. He appeared indifferent, but was he? From a few things which Paolo had said, she imagined that the Farenze fortune was enormous.

He looked down at her, his grey eyes smiling. 'Now, we have cleared away some of the tangled wood of the past, haven't we? Perhaps now you will consider my request.'

28

'Oh, you wanted me to cook dinner for you and the Countess?' She was deliberately obtuse, her tone bland. 'Where is the Countess, by the way?'

'She was kind enough to act for me in this little plot,' he said with a grin. 'As you long ago suspected! And what I have to ask you is nothing to do with dinner ... I want you to fly back to Italy with me this week, to see Paolo's father.'

'Never!' Her voice shook with burning indignation. 'No, never!'

He looked down at her sternly, his brows drawn together in a reproachful frown. 'He is an old man, soon to die. He has lost both his sons, and, whatever you may think of him, they were beloved sons. Why will you not grant him one small act of charity?'

'What charity did he and his family show me?' Nicola winced as she thought of Paul. She could lose him if she allowed the powerful Farenze clan to discover his existence. She must not permit them to suspect that there was a child. She turned on her heel. 'No, I'm sorry, it's impossible. Goodnight.'

He did not pursue her. She glanced back as she turned the corner, but there was no sign of him. But she was glad when she was back in the safety of the flat, despite the difficulty of fencing with Bess, who was bursting with questions at this sudden early return.

She rang Drew next day and told him that she had not cooked for the Countess after all. 'It was not required,' she added calmly.

'Aha!' Drew was instantly alert. 'So the Countess

was in the plot, eh? I am positively dying of curiosity, you know, my sweet. Won't you tell? It isn't the Mafia, is it?'

'Something along those lines,' she said flippantly.

'No! Really?' Drew was half fascinated, half incredulous.

'I'm kidding,' she said, and switched the subject for a few moments, before ringing off.

Each morning she awoke with a feeling of nervous anticipation. She hardly dared to go outside the front door in case she bumped into Domenico Farenze. But day succeeded day, and she saw no sign of him, and gradually her fears were lulled.

He had said that he was flying back to Italy soon. Surely, she thought, as she did the shopping a week later, he must have left England by now. She could relax again. He would have been in touch somehow if he had not accepted her word as final. He had had the look and manner of a man who acts decisively. Since he had not contacted her again she might assume that he had dismissed her from his memory.

The Farenze family, after all, had never shown any interest in Paolo's wife before. It was doubtful if they felt any now. Domenico Farenze had, presumably, acted on a sudden whim when he invited her to visit the Farenze home in Italy. He could not have been serious in believing that old Lorenzo Farenze could have any real desire to see his dead son's widow.

Well, he must be forgotten now, Nicola told herself,

smiling down at Paul as she pushed him along, singing to himself in a tuneless voice.

The sunshine was fragile, falling like the petals of a yellow rose on the rooftops and chimneys of London. Every now and then a passing cloud eclipsed the sun and the streets grew dull again. Then the cloud moved, and the faint gleams of gold re-awoke on the shop windows, the chrome of cars, the gently fluttering leaves of the plane trees.

As she turned to cross the road her heart was seized and twisted with fear. A tall, dark man was standing on the other side, staring across at her. Her vision was clouded briefly. Then her heart resumed its normal rhythm and she saw clearly. It was a total stranger.

The experience left its mark, however. She saw that, from now on, she would never be free of fear. Even if Domenico Farenze had returned to Italy by now, he might appear in London at any time. What if he visited the flat? Discovered the existence of her son?

She looked down at Paul's dark head in a passion of grief. They must never know about him. She knew enough about the family to know that they would attempt to gain possession of the boy—their money could buy them lawyers who would use every trick in the legal book on their behalf.

She wondered if she should visit a solicitor. She did not know enough about the law to know her rights. Could they do anything? Surely a mother, a widow, was safe enough. An English court would never allow a child to be taken away from its English mother—and, for all that his father had been Italian, Paul was English, for he had been born here, and registered as the child of a British subject.

All the same, she could not vanquish the fears which possessed her.

She had very little money, and the Farenze were wealthy. They had weapons which could be dangerous.

I must vanish again, she told herself. I'll leave London, take Paul into the country. She had sometimes looked at advertisements for a housekeeper which stated that one child would be accepted. She could find a job like that, take Paul with her.

What about Vanessa? She bit her lip. She was very fond of her sister. But if Vanessa, if anyone, knew where she had gone, it would be dangerous. Reluctantly, at the very back of her mind, she was aware that she suspected Vanessa of being slightly unreliable. Her sister was capable of spite, of occasional acts of dishonesty—not in the crude sense of stealing, but in the personal sense of breaking her word or deliberately performing some mean act. Vanessa, if she was bribed in some subtle way, might possibly tell the Farenze about Paul. Nicola had several times been hurt in the past when her sister did such things. She could not afford to trust Vanessa this time. Once Vanessa knew about the Farenze fortune which awaited Paul, she might be tempted.

She bought several magazines and took them back to the flat. She cooked Paul's lunch and fed him. Then, while he played on the floor with his dog on wheels, Spotty, she sat down with a cup of coffee and studied the advertisements for housekeepers.

Several seemed interesting. She ringed two of them in red and began a hunt for writing paper. Paul had got tired of Spotty and began to bang on his old saucepan with a wooden spoon, chanting loudly.

Someone rang the door bell. Nicola glanced at her watch. The baker? She found her purse and went to the door, Paul toddling at her heels with his saucepan precariously waving around his head.

She opened the door and then went white, her fingers clutching at the handle so that the metal burnt against her skin.

Domenico Farenze stared past her at the child, then his brows jerked together in a straight, black line.

Paul tugged at her skirt. 'Up, Mummy . . . up!'

Automatically she bent to pick him up, her arms clutching him convulsively.

He wriggled. 'Too tight . . .' Imperiously, his small face a faint echo of the frown which Domenico Farenze wore, he smacked her softly, rebuking her.

Domenico reached out towards him, lifted him firmly from her arms, ignoring Nicola's cry of bitter protest.

He held him away a little, studying him. The boy stared back in unconscious mimicry.

They were oddly alike. She saw the resemblance even as she resented it. No wonder Domenico had seemed familiar when she first saw him—he was the positive image of her own son, although Paul was so small and young. The softness of Paul's baby face would one day toughen into this strong, powerful mask.

'Paolo's eyes, his nose and jaw . . .' Domenico spoke softly, but anger burnt in every syllable.

She was silent. Their eyes met. He was, she saw, as pale as herself—but his pallor was the result of rage.

One of the women who lived on the floor above came past, staring curiously at them. Domenico, catching her sideways look, waited until she had gone, then said, 'Must we discuss this out here? Am I not to be admitted? You can have no further reason for keeping me away from your home.'

Nicola stepped back to permit him to enter the flat. He carried Paul into the sitting-room and sat down on a chair, with the child on his lap.

It was galling that the child so obviously found him fascinating. Galling—and astonishing. In the past Paul had been known to scream at the very sight of a strange man. Many of Vanessa's escorts had fled, shaking, after an encounter with Paul, and Vanessa had often complained bitterly about Paul's hostility towards her boyfriends.

Domenico Farenze, however, apparently found favour in the child's sight. Paul was busy inspecting every inch of this interesting newcomer; peering into his ears, lifting his collar to inspect his tie, fingering the gold watch on his tanned wrist and gently touching the dark hairs on the back of Domenico's hands.

Domenico allowed the child to inspect him while he

spoke, in a calm voice calculated not to alarm the boy, to Nicola.

'How old is he?'

'He's two,' she admitted.

The dark brows lifted. 'He was born after Paolo's death, I gather?'

She nodded.

'You did not see fit to tell his family that you were expecting a child?' The tone was withering.

'If any of his family had been sufficiently interested to come over to his funeral they would have seen for themselves. Paul was born a month later.'

'Paul?' The voice softened on the name, and the boy raised his head to give an abstracted smile, returning at once to his scrutiny of the watch.

Domenico looked at her sharply. 'You had no right to keep his birth a secret from his father's family!'

'They ignored me, why should I think they would be interested in my child?' Nicola stressed the possessive "my", looking at him with bitter eyes.

'You knew that we would be interested,' Domenico said calmly.

She laughed angrily. 'Only because he was a useful tool in your ambitions for the Farenze family! Do you think I wanted my child to get involved with all that stupid plotting, to be used by his grandfather as a pawn in some money game?'

'Ah!' Domenico shook his head. 'You resent the money?'

'I resent the way in which it's allowed to dominate your lives. I don't want that for my son.'

'You have no choice,' Domenico said softly.

Fear held her silent for a few seconds, then she swallowed and said hurriedly, 'Paul will never have anything to do with the Farenzes. I shall make certain of that. He is English, he was born in this country. He is my son—I'm his only legal guardian. There is nothing the Farenze family can do about that.'

Domenico shrugged. 'We shall see. We will get the best lawyers. Paul, after all, is the son of an Italian, and now the heir to a great fortune. I think his grandfather will fight for him. I know Lorenzo. Once he knows of Paul's existence he will want to have him brought to the Villa, to have him brought up as an Italian.'

'He is English,' she insisted.

The grey eyes held hers. Did she imagine it, or was there a glint of pity in them? 'Would Paolo, his father, have said so?'

The question was like a blow to the heart. She stared at him, wide-eyed and white-faced. He stared back in silence, watching her closely.

When she had first met Paolo one of the things which had drawn her to him had been his Italian gaiety, the charm and warmth which shone out of his face. He had been eager for a family, ecstatic when he knew she was going to have a child. She recalled, now, with a pang, how often Paolo had said that when the child had been born they would take it to Italy.

36

'*Cara*, we will take it to the Villa, to see the old Far-enzes in the rain; the bronze statues of his ancestors, all green with age, as if they wept green tears down their long Roman noses.'

Teasingly, she had said, 'Him? What if the child is a girl?'

Paolo had laughed, wickedly. 'Then I shall beat you and we shall try again, and that will be fun, too.' But she had known from his smile that whether girl or boy, the child would be wanted. Paolo adored babies. He was so unlike Englishmen. Where an Englishman ignored a pram in the street, Paolo would eagerly in-spect the inhabitant, admiring it noisily, delighting and astonishing the mother.

The sound of a key in the latch made her jump. Paul looked up and shouted, 'Tanty Van . . . Tanty Van!'

Vanessa, cross and weary after a long stint in the salons, paused in the door and hurriedly rearranged her face as she saw the stranger with her sister.

Domenico rose, a smile curling his mouth, and half bowed, waiting to be introduced.

'My sister, Vanessa Mayfield. Vanessa, this is Dom-enico Farenze.'

Vanessa looked startled, then curious. She smiled at him, holding out a languid hand. 'Related to Paolo, I gather? My sister is never very specific.'

He took her hand and raised it to his lips, kissing it lightly with a faint gesture of amusement. 'I am a second cousin—no closer than that, I'm afraid. Your family seems to produce beautiful girls, Miss Mayfield. Are there any more of you?'

'No, we are the only two samples,' said Vanessa with amused pleasure. 'But please, call me Vanessa.'

'Tanty Van ...' Paul murmured, tugging at Domenico's trouser leg in an attempt to re-establish ownership of this fascinating new friend.

Domenico grinned and picked him up, thus missing the flicker of irritation on Vanessa's beautiful face at Paul's nickname for her. She detested being called Van, and even Paul's age could not give him licence to use the loathed abbreviation.

When Domenico straightened, with Paul in his arms, Vanessa was all smiles again.

'Oh, Nicky love, I wonder if there's any salad in the fridge? I'm starving, but I'm so exhausted after work ...' She gave her sister a sweet, trailing smile.

Nicola nodded, resigned, and vanished to prepare a light meal. She made a fresh pot of coffee at the same time. When she returned to the sitting-room, it was to find Vanessa leaning back against the cushions of the sofa with her blonde curls spilled like sunshine on the green silk.

Paul was seated at the little coffee table, building brick palaces with Domenico Farenze.

'Where will you eat the salad?' Nicola asked her sister.

'Oh, I'm too tired to move. I'll have it on a tray here, thank you, Nicky.' Vanessa tilted her head to smile, looking even more like a Botticelli angel, her delicate features and pale complexion enhancing her fragility.

'Would you like some coffee, Mr Farenze?' Nicola made her voice cool yet not hostile. She had been thinking hard in the kitchen, and she was beginning, for the first time, to have some slight doubts about her decision to bring Paul up ignorant of his Italian inheritance.

Domenico's remark about Paolo's love for his home country had gone to her heart. She had forgotten many things, obsessed with her resentment of his family.

Domenico glanced up at her. The sun struck in across the room, picking out coppery lights in the fine dark hair. Her eyes were pure, cat green as she looked back at him, slanting and bright with dislike.

He smiled mockingly. 'Thank you. I would indeed like some coffee. Your coffee is excellent.'

Nicola could not find fault with the words. It was the tone which pricked at her. She knew, obscurely, that he was making fun of her in some devious way of his own.

When she returned with the coffee she found Vanessa listening to him intently, picking at her salad in a desultory fashion. She had eaten the lettuce and tomato, but was leaving most of the pink ham. Vanessa had little appetite for meat or fish. She was practically a vegetarian.

Nicola poured the coffee and took them each a cup. When she had seated herself on a small pink brocade chair, Domenico glanced at Vanessa. 'I have been telling your sister the background to my visit,' he said softly.

39

Nicola tensed. 'Oh?' She looked at her sister.

Vanessa did not quite meet her eyes. 'You haven't been strictly honest with us, have you, Nicky?'

The accusation took Nicola's breath away. After a pause, she asked indignantly, 'What are you talking about?'

'You never told us that Paul was the heir to the Farenze estate! You allowed us to believe that Paolo left you penniless. We've been so sorry for Paul, poor fatherless little boy—and all the time you knew very well that the Farenzes would jump at the chance to help you. Why have you let Paul live in this little box of a flat when he could have had a wonderful home in Italy?'

'I've always paid my way,' Nicola said in a quietly angry voice. 'I've never borrowed money from either you or Bess, have I?'

'We've babysat for you hundreds of times, though! Without payment!' Vanessa hurriedly added, 'Not that the money is really relevant, but our whole attitude to you was based on a lie. You told us nothing about Paolo's background, did you? You were always secretive, Nicky.'

'Paolo was my husband. What else should I have told you?'

'Were you ashamed of his Italian connections?' Domenico bit the words out.

'They were ashamed of me,' she retorted. 'You seem to forget that! Paolo told them about our marriage, but they ignored me. I told them about his death, and they ignored me. Why on earth should I have tried again? I know when to give up.'

'You were hurt,' said Vanessa, jumping up to kiss her. 'Your feelings were wounded ... but now Domenico has come to make amends, to give Paul everything he needs ... a home, toys, good school. A future to be proud of!'

Nicola pushed her coldly away. 'This is none of your business, Vanessa. Paul is my son. If his relations want to see him they'll have to come to England to do so.'

'How can you be so hard, so unjust?' Vanessa looked round at Domenico appealingly. 'I suppose it's because she has had to toughen up to face the world, to make a living for herself and Paul. She had no other choice after Paolo's death.'

'She has a choice now,' Domenico said softly. 'I want her to come to Florence, to the villa up in the hills of Tuscany, looking down over the vineyards and olives to the bright roofs of the greatest city of Italy. The Farenzes have lived there for hundreds of years. Paul is the last direct descendant of the old merchant princes of our house, and he must grow up in the ancestral home. His father's soul would desire it.'

Vanessa breathed a long sigh. 'Oh, Nicky, how can you hold out against that? You couldn't be so hard-hearted!'

Nicola gave her a glance of pure irritation. Domenico intercepted that look and grinned, his eyes gleaming with deep amusement.

Paul looked up, curious at the sudden silence.

Domenico knelt down beside him and smiled at the boy.

'Paul, would you like to come and pick ripe peaches from your own tree in a big garden? Would you like to splash in a fountain, throw pebbles from the top of a high, high tower down into a stream?'

Paul's eyes grew round. 'Yes, now!' He lifted his arms to Domenico. 'Go now!'

Domenico kissed him on the tip of his nose. 'Not now, Paul, but very soon.'

He looked round at Nicola, his grey eyes challenging. She stared back at him without answering, feeling the conflicting tug of different emotions—a desire to stay here, in the known security of England, and see Paul grow up here, and the new feeling, smothered and yet growing, that Paolo would have wished his son to grow up in Italy.

Almost pleadingly, she said, at last, 'I only want to do what's best for Paul.'

'I will book the seats for the first possible flight,' Domenico said. He glanced at Vanessa. 'I'm sure your sister will cope with any details which you have to leave unsolved.'

CHAPTER THREE

WHEN he had gone Vanessa gave Nicola a long, curious stare. 'Are you out of your skull, darling? Turning down that sort of money? I wouldn't mind if you had any sort of future to offer Paul, but you're as poor as a church mouse and always will be! Why, even when you marry into a wealthy family you go out of your way to offend them.'

'Paolo was brought up with all this wonderful background you've been telling me about,' said Nicola. 'He ran away from it!'

'Did he?' Vanessa laughed and shook her head. 'He carried it around with him, Nicky. You know that—if you'll only be honest for one minute!'

Nicola stood still, staring at her. 'What does that mean?'

Vanessa shrugged, the pale gold curls fluttering against her lifted hand as she began to brush her hair. 'Paolo had the sort of manner money always gives you —arrogance ...'

'He was not arrogant!' Nicola flared.

'Oh, it was courteous and gallant, but it was still arrogance. Domenico has the same manner.' Vanessa shot her sister a long, thoughtful look. 'You noticed that, didn't you?'

Nicola flushed. 'Paolo was nothing like Domenico!'

'Domenico is more reserved, rather more impressive —he has an air of authority, although he disguises it with courtesy. Perhaps all Italians are like that—the iron hand in the velvet glove?'

Nicola laughed. She remembered Paolo, watching her with an appealing face when he had been out all day at the races after swearing never to gamble again. Vanessa just did not know what she was talking about.

'Don't judge by appearances,' she said, a little forlornly. There had been other incidents in her brief married life which made her doubly wary now. She had told herself then, as she told herself now, that it had been the pernicious influence of his wealthy background which had so fatally weakened Paolo's character, and had killed him in the end.

Paul was never to be tempted in that way. He was to have a steady, sober British upbringing. Even a small child can learn to obey, to be polite, to be cheerful when he has to go to bed, instead of screaming to have his own way. Regular hours and quiet, gentle firmness were essential.

Nicola mentioned some of these points to Drew next day, when she called in to ask his advice, and he laughed helplessly.

'The British nanny to the rescue, eh? Character-building, if not empire-building? Nicky, you're a scream!'

'It isn't funny! I want Paul to be happy, and money seems to have the opposite effect.'

'Rather depends on the quantity and who's dishing it out, surely?' Drew was as near to serious as he ever achieved, his face wry. 'I mean, obviously we all need some money. We must eat. What you need, Nicky, is a solicitor.'

'What for?' She was puzzled.

'Advice, darling, advice!'

'I've told you—I don't want any money from the Farenzes. I shall allow Paul to visit them for a short time, then I'll bring him home again.'

'Nicky, if you're wise, you'll call in a solicitor, find out the legal position. If there are any doubts as to the guardianship of the child, have them ironed out before you go to Italy. Better to be safe than sorry.'

'How can there be any doubts? He was born here.'

'Of an Italian father!'

'But his father is dead, and I'm his guardian now.'

'By English law, yes, but I'd check Italian law if I were you. You don't want to run into any little local difficulties, do you?'

She stared at him in alarm. 'I suppose not. Yes, I'll do that, Drew!'

She visited a solicitor immediately, and he listened with interest to her story.

'Well, of course, there is little doubt as far as English law is concerned, and probably none in Italy, either, but there may be some legal document concerning the inheritance which covers the possibility ...'

'Would it be binding on me, though?'

'If your husband signed it, bequeathing his rights in his heirs to some executor; for instance his father—then this might be a danger to you.'

'What would it mean?' She was pale and alarmed.

The man shrugged. 'I couldn't say, since I don't even know if such a document exists. It would be likely, in the case of a large estate, that some such document was drawn up, to protect the estate in the event of the control over the heir passing out of family hands.'

'As it has?' She had a sudden premonition that this was more than just a vague possibility. Domenico had been so insistent, so sure of himself. 'Can I be protected against it?'

'While you're on English soil, of course. Your custody of the child would be of paramount importance since you are his mother. No court would agree to separating you for a purely financial motive.'

'But if he was taken to Italy?'

'Without your consent? We could undoubtedly fight the case in the Italian courts.'

'If I took him there myself? Once we were there, could he be taken away from me?'

'I'm sure not, but I could make certain of that, if you wish. I will ask for sight of any documents relating to the guardianship of the child before you agree to go to Italy.'

'Would you do that?' She gave him Domenico's telephone number at his hotel in London. He rang at once and made an appointment to see Domenico.

Domenico came to visit Paul again next morning. He gave Nicola a sharp look as she admitted him to the flat. 'I've just seen your solicitor. A trusting little creature, aren't you?'

She flushed. 'I don't trust you, or your family.'

His lip curled scornfully. 'And, despite all your brave talk, there is the question of the Farenze fortune to be investigated!'

Her eyes flashed. 'I meant what I said—the money means nothing to me! I wouldn't touch a penny of Farenze money. I can earn everything I need. I'm a good cook.' She eyed him with biting contempt. 'I may not be socially acceptable to the Farenzes, but a good cook can always earn a living, especially these days, when good cooks are hard to find. There are twice as many jobs as there are applicants. I can live handsomely on what I earn.'

'A long speech,' Domenico drawled. 'Methinks the lady doth protest too much!'

Paul looked from one to the other of them in dismay. He did not like raised voices and angry expressions. Like most children, he was sensitive to the atmosphere around him, and now he plucked at Nicola's skirt. 'Mummy'... Mummy!'

She looked down, saw his worried frown, and bent to pick him up in her arms. Forcing a bright smile, she said, 'I'll make some coffee for our visitor, shall I, Paul? And cold milk for you?'

'Uncle ...' Paul broke into relieved smiles, holding out his hand to Domenico. 'Uncle, carry me!'

Domenico took him, raised him to his shoulders and let him ride there, crowing with delight and holding tightly to the thick dark hair.

As Nicola made the coffee, watching the two of them, she thought that it would have been like this if Paolo had lived. He would have been a doting, indulgent father.

Domenico caught her passing frown of pain, and misunderstood. Giving Paul his saucepan and spoon to play with in a corner, he said sharply, 'Too bad you don't like to see me with the boy—you will have to get used to it. I intend to see a great deal of him from now on! I am the nearest thing he has got to an uncle.'

'I wasn't even thinking about you,' she cried. 'I was thinking about ...' Her voice broke and she turned away.

He caught her shoulders and spun her to face him, his fingers biting into her flesh. She stood, head bowed, tears burning in her eyes but unshed.

One hand roughly forced her chin up so that he could see her face clearly.

'Did you take a vow of perpetual widowhood?' His tone was cruelly mocking. Nicola stared at him in dislike.

'I don't expect you to understand!'

'Try me! I am not so lacking in perception!'

'Paolo was his father—a father who never saw him!' The tears fell, now, as the words expressed what she had only felt before. The salt stung her eyes, her skin, her lips. She felt a rending anguish, then a strange, drowning relief.

His hand came up again, a handkerchief firmly wiped her face, as if she was a child. She felt weak, her instinct was suddenly to lean upon him, cling to him. Her breath came raggedly. She could hear her heart beating faster.

Slowly, quiveringly, she glanced up at him through her lashes, and found his grey eyes fixed on her face. Cold anger hardened his face. He was frowning, his lips tight.

'I will not be a substitute for Paolo,' he said icily.

She gasped. Her hand swung up, hit his cheek before he had had notice of her intention. His fingers caught her wrist, dug viciously, pulled her hand down against her side.

'You forget the child,' he murmured between clenched teeth. 'And next time you feel the need for a man, pick someone else.' His eyes glinted angrily at her. 'Someone who is too blind to realise that you are only looking for a pale imitation of what you had with your husband. No man of any spirit would marry a girl so obviously obsessed with a dead man, or permit himself to be used as a stand-in for another man.'

'You ... you ...' Nicola stammered helplessly in her fury, the bitter depth of her humiliation. The fact that part of what he said was too painfully true made her anger with him worse. For a few weak moments she had almost abandoned her sense of reality, almost allowed

49

herself to pretend that this dark stranger who looked so like Paolo was, truly, her dead husband. It had been a ridiculous piece of folly. She could not, now, even understand what had made her behave in such a degrading fashion.

She made the coffee in silence, poured him a cup and vanished into her own room, leaving him to play with Paul alone. In her room, she looked at herself in the mirror, saw the hair loose around her pale face, the tearstains on cheek and eyelid, the faint pink around her eyes.

She groaned. How could she have behaved like that? It was despicable.

She would never be able to forget it, never be able to forgive Domenico for having been quick enough to comprehend the emotions passing through her. He had been too clever, too perceptive.

He is dangerous, she thought angrily. How can I bear to see him, feeling that he reads my thoughts so easily?

She sank on to the bed, covering her face. It was humiliating to feel oneself so transparent.

Vanessa, surprisingly, arrived back home early, explaining that she had a slight headache and the salon was so stuffy. 'I needed some air . . .'

'Did Madame Annette mind your leaving early?' Nicola was disturbed. Vanessa had been back early three times this week.

Domenico, stretched out on the sofa, his long legs crossed in front of him, stared mockingly at Vanessa as, a little pink-cheeked, she shook her head.

'I'll fix you a salad for lunch,' Nicola said.

'Why don't I take you out somewhere?' Domenico asked lightly.

Nicola stood still, looking from one to the other. Vanessa gave a charming little start of surprise, laughed, bit her little finger as she pretended to consider the suggestion.

'That's very sweet of you—I eat so little!' She fluttered her lashes at him, her Botticelli face full of gentle sweetness.

'I'll eat enough for both of us,' he promised, a trifle dryly.

She giggled. 'Well, thank you, then, Domenico! I'd love to have lunch with you.'

Nicola walked abruptly into the kitchen. It suddenly occurred to her that this was just what Vanessa had been angling for—it was why she had come home early so often since Domenico started coming to the flat to see Paul.

Why didn't I realise before that Vanessa was interested in him? I'm a fool.

Was he interested in Vanessa, though? He was not a man one could read easily. That cool manner of his disguised far too much.

She began to prepare a salad for her own lunch. Paul had eaten his, and was taking his afternoon nap. He ate his lunch early. A sound behind her made her turn her head. Domenico lounged against the door.

He returned her cold glance. 'To revert to our earlier discussion for a moment, I have put your solicitor in touch with our solicitor in London. They will sort this out between them. I have agreed that there be some sort of agreement that Paul is in your custody, and that Lorenzo and myself will not seek guardianship in any way during your lifetime. They'll draw up some document for us both to sign.'

'And Lorenzo Farenze?'

'He will sign, too, of course.'

'Have you been in touch with him yet? Does he know ...'

'About Paul? Yes, I have spoken to him on the telephone. He was ...' His voice broke off suddenly. He shrugged, lifting his shoulders in an alien gesture. After a moment he went on crisply, 'Lorenzo had thought himself without descent—his sons dead without issue. Suddenly to hear that he had a grandson ...'

She saw that he was striving to keep all emotion from his face and voice. Was he a man who distrusted emotion? Even feared it, perhaps?

'I hope he understands that Paul is not to stay in Italy for ever? I have not promised any more than that he may visit his grandfather. That is all.'

He gave her a look as inflexible as steel, his mouth parted in a dry, sardonic smile. 'We will cross these bridges when we come to them. Let the old man be happy for a while. My main fear was that, in giving him such news out of the blue, I might bring on a heart attack.'

'Joy never kills anyone,' she said flatly.

'You are a stranger to joy,' he retorted, his glance mocking and scornful. 'Hiding in the shadows of life, turning your face from the sun—how would you know anything about joy? If you were not a mother, you would doubtless have taken the veil.' He moved closer, staring down at her. 'Is there blood in your veins, you chilly little creature, or are you frozen for ever inside the green ice of those eyes of yours?'

The click of Vanessa's heels along the corridor made her jump back from him. She had been half hypnotised by the soft Italian voice—he had lapsed into Italian while he spoke, and she suddenly realised that he used Italian whenever he was talking intimately. Was that because it was the language of his heart, the tongue he heard inside his head even when he spoke English? She herself spoke Italian fluently. She had learnt it at school. It was her knowledge of Italian which had brought her into Paolo's life.

Paolo had been staying at the hotel in which she was working during her last vacation at college. She had taken a temporary summer job while waiting for the results of her final examinations. Finding that she spoke Italian quite well, the proprietor had used her as an interpreter in cases of emergency.

One day Paolo had had a bowl of hot soup spilled over his new suit in the dining-room. He had exploded into fountains of excitable Italian.

Baffled and horrified, the head waiter sent for Nicola from the kitchen. Prettily, dimpling and soothing, she had talked Paolo out of his rage. Faced with a pretty young girl who spoke his language, he was not difficult to calm.

She had dinner with him on her night off that week. She walked with him in the mornings. He wrote her ardent little notes. Their courtship had been sudden, feverish and swept everything else out of their heads.

Paolo cabled home that he was marrying her. They waited for an answer, but all that came was a brief, icy note telling him never to bring her back to Florence. The family would never forgive him.

'My father does not even write himself,' Paolo said bitterly. 'This is not his writing!'

'Perhaps we should wait,' Nicola had murmured unhappily. 'I don't want to come between you and your family, dearest.'

Paolo had seized her in his arms. 'You are all my family, now. My darling ...

That afternoon she was persuaded to give up her job. Paolo bought a special licence and they were married so soon that she barely had time to consider exactly what she was doing. They were both of age. There was no reason why they should wait, Paolo urged her. Blind with love, she followed him.

She sat, staring out of the window, sunk in reverie, quite forgetting Domenico.

Vanessa joined him, slipped a hand into his elbow and looked up at him in surprise as he made no movement.

He was watching Nicola with eyes so cold that Vanessa looked almost alarmed. His lean dark face was as rigid as carved wood. The taut mouth and jaw, the clenched teeth, all spoke of icily controlled rage.

Vanessa was puzzled. What was wrong? She coughed, and he started. She saw a shutter slip down over the grey eyes. He turned slowly, gathering his wits, and gave her a smile.

'You look quite charming, my dear girl. A breath of spring—a true Primavera!'

She lifted bewildered blue eyes. 'A true what?'

'You do not know the Botticelli painting? It is a painting of the essence of rebirth, of springtime; girls dancing in a wood, the Graces, nymphs in fragile gossamer dresses—and in the foreground, a girl like you, slender and graceful, with flowers strewn on her gown and in her golden hair! You must have seen it somewhere. It is one of the most famous paintings in the world.' His voice had been warm with mellifluous Italian enthusiasm as he spoke, but Vanessa carefully noticed that his eyes watched her sister over her head.

Was he interested in Nicola? she pondered coolly. But if he was, why did he look so coldly at her? Had they just had a row? Yes, she decided, that was it. There had been an atmosphere you could cut with a knife whenever she had seen them together. They just did not hit it off.

Good thing, she decided thoughtfully. Nicky was not quite in her own class, perhaps, but she had a certain something. Vanessa wasn't quite sure exactly what it was that her sister did have—she only knew that it could be pretty potent at times. She had lost boys to Nicky in the past—and without Nicky apparently lifting a finger to achieve it.

This time it's different, she thought, as she and Domenico left. This man is different. I'm no longer as young as I would like to be—in my profession one is past it at twenty-five. I only have a few good years left in this business.

'What exactly do you do for a living?' She smiled up at him as she asked the question, softening the curtness of the words.

'I work in the business, of course,' he said in some surprise.

'What business?' She frowned.

'Why, surely Paolo must have talked about it?'

Vanessa shrugged. 'He talked about Italy, but never about your family.'

Domenico's face tightened. 'I see.'

'Don't look so hurt,' she said softly. 'I think Paolo knew that Nicky hated to hear him talk about his home. She felt guilty because he had given it up for her.'

'You think so?' He looked sharply at her.

'I'm sure of it. I know Nicky.' She laughed softly. 'I've known her all my life, after all. She was totally wrapped up in Paolo—the sun shone out of him for her. When he was killed she was like a walking ghost for months. If it hadn't been for little Paul I think she would have died herself. Only the fact that she had him to look after pulled Nicky through that time.'

'But Paolo died two years ago—more than two years ago! It will soon be three years!'

Vanessa sighed. 'Yes—she's amazingly faithful, isn't she? I don't think I could be quite as single-minded as Nicky.'

'You believe she still loves Paolo?' His voice was curt.

'She's never even looked at another man since.'

He nodded slowly. 'She is walled up with the dead —as I had thought myself! I am sorry to hear you confirm my suspicions.'

She shot him a wary look. 'Sorry?'

His eyes widened. 'But yes ...' His voice grew suddenly very Italian. 'It is not healthy for a girl so young to think only of a man who has been dead for two years.'

Vanessa sat cross-legged on the carpet in the sitting-room that night, brushing her hair, her blue eyes fixed on her sister. Bess was sewing a neat little jacket for Paul, on the other side of the room. She made a great many clothes for him. She enjoyed designing clothes for children.

'Do you know much about the Farenze family, Nicky?' Vanessa asked.

'Very little,' Nicky replied indifferently.

'They're stinking rich,' said Vanessa.

Nicky looked at her without speaking.

Vanessa flushed a little. 'Well, why didn't you tell us about that? What else haven't you told us? You never mentioned that they were wine exporters, did you?

57

That Dom is here on business, selling wine to this country? That that was what Paolo was doing over here in the first place before he threw up his job with the family to take that terrible job as an interpreter?'

'You have been busy, haven't you?' Nicky was angry. 'You must have had fun extracting all that information.'

'Why did Paolo give up his job? Because he resented the way they treated him and the way they ignored your marriage?' Vanessa smiled unpleasantly. 'Or was there another reason?'

Nicky looked at her sister with resentful irritation. 'Why must you keep talking about this? Change the subject.'

'Paolo couldn't, of course, have embezzled company funds to finance his gambling?'

Nicky froze, her eyes widening. 'What? Is that what Domenico Farenze told you?' Her voice was high and tense.

Bess put down her sewing and looked at her anxiously.

'Vanessa, stop this! You're upsetting Nicky. Don't listen to that nonsense, Nicky. Vanessa is only trying to get at you.'

'I'm only trying to clear away a few of the veils she's hung around her statue of Paolo on his pedestal,' Vanessa said tartly. 'I think it's time Nicky admitted the truth to herself. Paolo was no angel. He gambled, he lied—and he killed himself when he drove that sports car of his the wrong way down the motorway. Come to that, he damn near killed a few other people at the same time. If that other car hadn't managed to avoid him there would have been other graves in the cemetery now.'

Bess sprang to her feet as Nicky ran out of the room. 'My God, Vanessa, I sometimes think you hate your sister! Why did you have to drag all that out just now?'

'I'm a little tired of Saint Paolo and his good works. Nicky has the chance of the good life if only she'll snap out of this. She could be one of the richest women in Italy—live in a fabulous medieval villa and wear the Farenze emeralds.' Vanessa's blue eyes had a starry, rapt look and her voice was breathless. 'Why the hell did Nicky have to be such a fool!'

Bess looked at her contemptuously. 'You really mean, why didn't I get the chance of all that? You would jump at it, wouldn't you, Van?'

'Don't call me that! And why shouldn't I want the good things of life? Dom told me tonight that, as the widow of Paolo Farenze, Nicky is entitled to wear a necklace of emeralds as big as postage stamps, square-cut and set with diamonds.' Vanessa bit her thumbs helplessly. 'And Nicky couldn't care less!' Her voice wailed in despair. 'She couldn't care less!'

'So, in order to persuade her to accept what the Farenzes have to offer, you set about destroying her memory of her husband? How low can you sink?' Bess looked at her with disgust.

Vanessa hardly heard her. 'Nicky has got to change her attitude. She must realise that it's ridiculous to blame the Farenzes. Paolo was as much to blame as

59

them. She mustn't alienate them. She must forget Paolo.'

'You aren't thinking of going to Italy, too, are you?' Bess asked in sudden dismay.

Vanessa looked at her defiantly. 'Why not? Nicky will need moral support.'

'Moral support!' Bess snorted. 'You're joking, of course!'

'Make fun of me as much as you like,' Vanessa said with a toss of the light golden curls. 'But Dom has already said that I shall be very welcome at the Villa Farenze. I'm Nicola's only surviving relative, after all. It's a good idea for me to meet her new family. They'll be able to see just what sort of background she comes from—and they can forget all that stupid nonsense about her being a cook.'

'She is a cook, though,' said Bess in mock innocence. 'And a damned good one, too.'

Vanessa threw her an irritated glance. She's a Cordon Bleu cook, yes, but it's only a sort of hobby.'

'Come off it, Van,' Bess teased. 'They aren't going to swallow that—and Nicky will never allow you to tell lies about her. Her pride would choke here.'

'Nicky's pride makes me sick,' Vanessa snapped. 'She ought to have some sort of brain surgery. She's a certifiable lunatic! In her place . . .'

'We all know what you would do in her place,' Bess murmured sardonically. 'Grab everything that was going and run for the nearest exit!'

'I'm not that mercenary,' Vanessa said crossly. 'I just

feel that Nicky should accept what's hers by right.'

'And you're going with her to make sure she does accept it, even if you have to twist her arm to make certain?'

Vanessa's lovely face set in grim determination. Had any of her admirers seen her in that mood they would have been taken aback to see the tenacity and strength beneath her delicately feminine features.

'I'm going to Italy with her, and nothing is going to stand in my way,' she murmured, half to herself.

CHAPTER FOUR

PAUL was sick in the car as they drove from the airport to the villa at Florence. The flight had upset him a little, but the long drive had a far worse effect, and by the time they had reached the green Tuscan hills he was whimpering and a pale yellow colour.

'Keep him away from me!' Vanessa shrieked as he was sick, drawing her elegant white skirt away from his vicinity.

To Nicky's surprise, Domenico was gentle and efficient in that emergency. He handled Paul calmly, cleaned up the car seat and was philosophical about the ruin of his own trousers.

When Nicky tried to apologise, he said dismissively, 'Forget it! He couldn't help it.'

'You must have your suit cleaned and send me the bill,' she said ruefully.

The grey eyes narrowed. 'I said forget it!' The tone was like a slap in the face.

She flushed and fell silent. They had been met at the airport by a uniformed chauffeur. His formal courtesy made her feel like an impostor, in her simple yellow linen travelling suit, as she followed him to the car with Paul in her arms. Domenico had sat in the back with Paul, and Vanessa had pleaded to sit there too, claiming that she always felt nervous at driving in the front seat. Nicola had given her an amused smile, seeing through this rather blatant attempt at dividing them.

Her own mind was far too occupied with what was to come, the first meeting with Lorenzo and the rest of the Farenze clan.

She tried to recall all that Paolo had said about them, but he had really said too little, and what he had told her had been so scrappy.

His mother, of course, had died years ago, but his father had not married again. He had married so late in life, and was a man who found personal relationships hard, as far as she could guess from what little she knew about him. Lorenzo was an old man now, weakened by illness, yet still no doubt as awe-inspiring as he had sounded when Paolo spoke of him.

Vanessa was asking Domenico questions along the same line. 'Who else will we meet besides your uncle?'

'My own mother,' he said. 'My father is dead. My mother lives at the Villa. Then there is my cousin Bianca—she lives there, too.'

'Do the whole family live at the Villa?' Vanessa laughed in a brittle fashion, her eyes narrowed. 'What does Bianca do?'

'She helps to run the house, and does secretarial work for Lorenzo. She is a remote cousin, actually. Her parents live in Rio de Janeiro, but she gave up travelling with them to come back to Italy and work for Lorenzo.'

'She's an only child?'

He shook his head, his face hardening. 'She has a brother.'

Vanessa watched him curiously. 'You make that sound ominous!'

'Leo is an idle layabout,' he said tersely.

Vanessa laughed. 'Don't tell me he lives at the Villa, too?'

'Lorenzo is foolish enough to permit him to live in the old watch-tower. Leo pretends to paint there.'

'Pretends?' Vanessa asked, raising an eyebrow.

'He is no more an artist than I am,' snapped Domenico.

Dreamily, Nicola murmured, 'Portrait of a Happy Family!'

Domenico leaned back against the leather upholstery, his gaze on the back of her shining dark head. She glanced into the driving mirror above her, and their eyes met. His were narrowed to steely points of light, hers wide, innocent, with hidden contempt in their green depths.

'No doubt you will prefer Leo's version of himself,' he drawled. 'He sees himself as the second Michelangelo. But be careful, Nicola, he demands tribute from the worshippers at his shrine. Beautiful girls flock to kneel at his feet in homage, and Leo expects them to be unstinting in their admiration.'

Vanessa laughed. 'He'll be disappointed where Nicky is concerned—she isn't susceptible.'

'No?' Again the grey eyes sought Nicola's in the mirror. 'I wonder. Even grief must have an end.'

Nicola turned her head aside, her lids flicking down over her green eyes, and stared at the distant prospect of dusty roads, tapering cypress and green olive groves. It was like the backcloth to some old Italian painting, brought to life by magic, lacking only the Madonna and Child for the foreground. Instead of a stable and a star, she saw the gleam of chromium and bright paint, the tourists in the coach in front, drinking from cans and eating crisps.

Then they turned up a steep hill, between crumbling old walls, climbing steadily along a deserted, narrow lane. The snarl of the traffic was left far behind. They were the only vehicle in sight until they came upon a cart, pulled by a weary donkey, plodding along in front of them. The driver, in blue shirt and jeans, grinned and waved as he pulled aside into a convenient opening.

A little further up the wall again opened and a wide gateway showed before them. Snarling lions sat, crouched on their hind legs, paws upraised above carved stone shields, upon the gate posts.

'The Farenze lion,' Domenico said to Paul with a quick smile, gesturing to them.

Paul's blank look brought a look of reproach for Nicola. 'You have not told him about the Farenze lion?' asked Domenico in a deep, stern voice.

She shrugged. 'Told him what?'

'Paolo never mentioned it?'

She thought back. 'I'm not sure . . .' There had really been so little time—they had had so many other things to talk about. She gave Domenico a defiant look. 'Paolo and I had better things to do than discuss his family history all day.'

His black brows jerked together. A cruel, biting look spat from the grey eyes, and the firm mouth thinned.

He looked down at Paul. 'The first Farenze was a rich merchant many hundreds of years ago. He travelled to the Far East. The king of that country gave him a lion cub as a present, and when he came back to Italy the cub came too. It followed him everywhere, like a pet dog. When it grew large, it stayed faithful and loving to him. It protected him when he went hunting, and when an enemy attempted to kill him, the lion sprang at his assailant and drove him away. For years the lion went everywhere with him. Then one day he went to a banquet alone, and his enemies served him poisoned wine. He ran from the banquet, dying. The lion sat outside, waiting for him. The Farenze fell at his lion's feet, and the beast sat there, growling, refusing to let anyone come near.'

Paul was breathless, wide-eyed. 'Then what happened?' he gasped in excitement.

'His master's little daughter was persuaded to come and lead the beast into its cage so that the Farenze could be buried. They held a splendid funeral procession. Everyone suspected that the Farenze had been poisoned, but they could not prove it, nor did they know who had done it, for he had several enemies. During the funeral procession the widow of the dead man insisted that the lion follow the coffin, led by a golden chain held by the little daughter. Suddenly the lion sprang at one of the mourners and killed him with one blow. Dying, the man cried out his guilt—he had poisoned the Farenze!'

Paul's mouth was a perfect circle of astonishment and total belief. 'How did the lion know?'

Domenico shrugged. 'Who can say? He may have suspected him by coincidence, or he may have smelt the guilt on him. Or the Farenze may have whispered his murderer's name as he died.'

'What happened to the lion?'

'He was kept, an honoured guest, in his cage until he died, and, as you see, he was adopted as the emblem of our house. The lion of Farenze is famous throughout the world. It can be seen on shields throughout the villa.'

Paul stared up at the gates. 'He looks fierce and brave.'

Domenico touched the boy's dark head with one gentle hand. 'You are going to meet another such in a moment . . .'

Paul's eyes grew wider. 'A lion?'

Domenico shook his head. 'Your grandfather. As the head of the family, he bears the title Lion of Farenze— it has always been so for centuries. It used to have some meaning in the world. We are poorer now, and have no power, but the title remains as a reminder of what the family expects from him who is the head of it—courage, gallantry, fidelity.'

Paul looked half bewildered, his soft baby features taut with anticipation.

'He's too young to understand you,' Nicola said sharply. 'I won't have him loaded down with ancient history at his age—all these empty, forgotten legends are meaningless now. This is the twentieth century, not the Middle Ages.'

Domenico's arrogant features tightened. For a second he looked more medieval than the house towards which they sped. His cruel, frightening glare made her draw back. 'I want him soaked in his family history,' he said in tones of soft menace. 'Saturated in it! He will one day inherit this, after all. The earlier he learns about the past from which he springs, the more likely it is that he will understand himself. We are all rooted in our past. We draw nourishment from it, as flowers do, and turn our faces to the sun like them, to find the strength to reproduce that past in the future.'

'What,' Vanessa demanded, 'are you talking about? What sun?'

His grey eyes were suddenly wickedly amused. 'The sun of love, of passion—what else?'

She laughed. 'Oh, now we're on a subject I can understand.'

The car was moving at a smooth pace along a gravelled drive between high, clipped hedges. Through gaps in the hedges now and then they caught a glimpse of a formal Italian garden, the garden of which Paolo had often spoken to her.

Box hedges, cypresses green and elegant, paths which were slippery with moss and a few scattered weeds, rain-greened statues of muscled gods and lightly draped goddesses who were, she knew, in reality statues of past members of the family; there they all were, as Paolo had described.

The garden was a cool, shadowy place, a little sad, as though it would have liked to blaze with colour under the hot Italian sun. The few flowers trailed elegantly from fine stone urns, or were massed together in painted wooden troughs along walls.

Beyond them, white and walled in from the sun, stood the Villa. Built in the sixteenth century, around a central courtyard, it turned away from the dazzling light and heat, providing a cool place for the languors of the day. The walls had few windows. Most of the rooms looked out on the courtyard.

More of the naked gods stood along the parapet above them, most of them defaced by time and weather. A hand, a leg, even a head would have vanished over the years. Birds used them as perching posts. They were spotted with moss and even a few brave plants which had taken root in cracks in the marble.

Nicky saw, from Vanessa's face, that her sister was deeply disappointed. She had been expecting a magnificent palazzo, no doubt, and found only a large country villa, in beautiful grounds, but so old that now it was crumbling away minute by minute. Time had cracked the stone, crumbled the masonry, sown the seeds of destruction everywhere.

Yet the old house had still a sort of splendour. Mellow, dignified, it looked on the face of time and was not disturbed. It was dying slowly, inch by inch, and in its decay it was perhaps even more beautiful than in its heyday.

As she gazed up at it, her eyes dreamy with appreciation, she felt Domenico's piercing look, and looked round to meet it.

He was staring at her, speculative, questioning, almost hopeful. Involuntarily, she smiled.

'It's lovely,' she said softly.

His expression lightened. The grey eyes smiled back.

'Oh, yes,' Vanessa cried instantly, not to be outdone. 'I'm bowled over! Fantastic! It's so ...' She sought for the right word and failed to find it. Weakly, she finished, 'So ... old ...'

Nicky's eyes danced. Domenico, watching her rather than Vanessa, grinned. 'Yes,' he said solemnly to Vanessa, 'it is old, isn't it?'

The car shot through an archway into the central courtyard. The dazzling whiteness of the scene outside gave way to cool shadows. They climbed out of the car and turned as someone came out from under a wooden terrace-roof.

Plump, black-eyed and black-haired, the woman was dressed in the same sombre hue. Her sallow skin had never known the touch of cosmetics, Nicky instinctively

70

guessed. Her hair was drawn back from her round face in a tight, neat bun, scraped away out of sight so that her face looked oddly naked. She was middle-aged, soft-stepping, her black eyes hostile as she looked at the two girls.

'Angelina,' said Domenico, moving to kiss her cheek. 'How are you, *cara mia*?'

She accepted his kiss, her face softening. Over his shoulder her eyes alighted on Paul, riding on Nicky's shoulder, his small head drooping wearily.

She pushed Domenico aside and came to Nicola. 'Give me the boy,' she said in a hoarse, harsh voice.

Nicola's hands tightened on her son. She frowned. The stab of the black eyes was full of cold hostility, but she smiled coolly at the other woman. 'Thank you, but I think I'd better keep him with me for the moment. He's not used to strangers.'

'Let Angelina take him,' said Domenico. 'You are tired. There is no need to be alarmed. She was Paolo's nurse—she knows very well how to look after children.'

Nicky lookd quickly at the sallow face. Angelina stared back, unsmiling, and attempted to take Paul from her again.

'No!' Nicola said sharply. 'He's in a strange country, among strange people. That's enough for him to cope with at present. He needs the security of my presence for a little while until he's used to being here.' She looked at Angelina again, and spoke in Italian. 'If you will show me the room you have prepared for us, I will take him up there myself.'

71

Angelina looked surprised. 'She speaks our tongue,' she said to Domenico.

He nodded. 'Show her the room for the boy, Angelina. They are both of them exhausted.'

Suddenly the quiet courtyard erupted with sound as a door banged and an old man came out, the stick on which he leaned clicking along the cobbles. Heavy and bowed, with a great noble head framed in silvery hair, he stared at Nicola and the child for a moment, his black eyes shining in the lined map of his face.

In husky Italian, he said, 'The boy ...'

Domenico turned, with outstretched hands, to take Paul from his mother, but Nicola shook her head firmly. She walked slowly across the courtyard and stood in front of the old man, looking at him calmly.

'Paul,' she said gently, 'this is your grandfather.'

The little boy raised his weary head and his eyes, shaded by drooping lashes, looked curiously at the newcomer.

Lorenzo Farenze stared back at him, taking in the dark hair and eyes, the fine features and straight, Italian nose.

'Are you the Lion of Farenze?' Paul asked eagerly.

Lorenzo shifted his glance to Nicola and a faint smile touched the corners of his mouth. 'So? He has heard the family legends already. That is good.' He smiled at Paul, nodding his leonine head. '*Si*, Paolo, I am the Lion of Farenze—but one day, little one, you will be the Lion. Would you like that?'

Paul considered the novel idea. He was pleased. 'Yes,' he said thoughtfully, 'I would like to be the Lion of Farenze. I'll bite people.'

Lorenzo threw back his head and laughed loudly. Nicola gave Domenico a bitter look.

'It seems my son has inherited a fatal family characteristic,' she said.

Looking down at her with mocking amusement, he said softly, 'Ah, but we are faithful, and where we love we are tenacious. That you should appreciate!'

'Give me the boy,' Lorenzo demanded, cutting into this talk. 'I will take him to his room.'

'He always sleeps in my room,' Nicola said quickly.

Lorenzo lifted indifferent shoulders. 'That is as it should be—he will need care in the night, yes? But that was in England. Here in Italy there is Angelina, who has nursed his father, and is aching to watch over the little one.'

Nicola politely insisted, 'It's very kind of her, but I prefer to keep him with me.'

Lorenzo turned a cold, arbitrary countenance towards her. 'That is no longer suitable. You are the widow of my son. Here, there are servants to do these tasks.'

'No one but myself will do anything for Paul unless I wish it,' she said quietly.

The black eyes spat at her, demanding capitulation. Without flinching she stared back, her mouth set in a straight line.

Lorenzo gave a growl. 'What is this, Domenico? She is stubborn as a mule! In a pretty girl this is not expected . . .'

Domenico laughed. 'She is English, remember. The breed is stubborn and independent. It is maddening, but there is nothing to be done for the moment but accept it.'

'Have you no pretty coaxing wiles, child?' Lorenzo shook his head. 'That is how a woman gets her own way—by pleading and pleasing, not with this defiant pigheadedness.'

Vanessa laughed, drawing the attention to herself. 'I'm afraid you won't get coaxing from Nicky. She has always despised that approach.'

Lorenzo looked at her in amused interest. 'But . . . what a beauty? Who is this?'

'Nicola's sister, Vanessa,' Domenico told him, and introduced them.

Lorenzo bowed over Vanessa's hand in a courtly gesture. '*Bella signorina*,' he murmured. He looked from her to her sister. 'You are not alike, you two? You have the head of a Botticelli madonna, while your sister has a head of black silk, with lights of fire . . .'

Vanessa laughed softly. 'How very apt! You are clever, *signore*. You read characters at sight.'

'Is there fire in your sister?' Domenico asked, his grey eyes flicking over Nicky. 'I thought it was all ice behind those green eyes.'

Vanessa frowned. 'Nicky has only ever been impulsive once—when she met Paolo.'

'Ah, she was on fire for our Paolo!' Lorenzo seemed amused by this.

Domenico's mouth thinned. Sardonically, he said, 'What a riddle she is—this girl with lights of fire on her head and ice in her eyes!'

Vanessa wound her hand through his arm. 'Nicky is waiting to take Paul to bed. Poor pet, she's tired.' The tone was gentle, but Vanessa was irritated.

They moved inside the house, and found themselves in a lofty marble-floored hall, from which a staircase wound upwards into shadowy regions. A girl stood waiting for them, her hands folded before her in a classical attitude of patience which was belied by the angry set of her red mouth.

'Ah, Bianca *cara*, come and meet Paolo's wife and son!'

Lorenzo's voice was warm, but uneasy, as though he half expected the reaction he indeed got.

'Am I to curtsey to the new lady of this house?' The voice snapped like a curving whip and the black eyes bit at Nicola across the hall.

Lorenzo grew scarlet with rage. 'What is this? How dare you speak like this in front of strangers!'

'Oh,' the girl mocked, 'they are strangers, are they? But strangers who must be placated, be made much of ... almost worshipped ... for they bring you a new heir for your fortune, don't they?' She curtsied deeply, her lips bitterly smiling. 'Welcome to the Villa Farenze, *signora*. Before you came we were secure in our little company. Suddenly all is changed—the despised ser-

75

vant girl who stole our Paolo has magically provided us with a new heir, a wonderful boy to carry on our family name! So all the hate is forgotten overnight. The servant girl is to be transformed into a lady ... flattered, cherished, spoilt.'

'Bianca, stop this!' Domenico strode forward to seize her shoulders, but she avoided him. Her black eyes were full of unshed tears as she glared at Nicola. Bianca was slender, golden-skinned like a peach, with smooth black hair and an exquisite little face. But now she looked like an avenging angel as she flung her insults.

'I am wicked, am I not? I speak the truth—and that is always wrong in this house!'

'You speak nonsense,' he retorted.

'Are you, too, won over to her? Do you forget the grief that marriage caused us all? Poor Barbara ... rejected by Paolo when it had been understood for so long that she was to be his wife? Think of her shame and grief—my best, my dearest friend, who should have been part of this family!'

Nicola looked at Lorenzo. Quietly she said, 'This is no scene for Paul to witness. I would like to go to my room.'

Angelina nodded and beckoned. Nicola followed her, ignoring Bianca's raging weeping. She glanced down once as she turned the bend in the stair and saw Domenico with his arms around the other girl, stroking the black hair gently, his mouth an inch above her bowed head.

Angelina looked down, too, and smiled. 'Ah, that

one will be tamed soon, when Domenico marries her and teaches her the purpose of these passionate urges she feels ...'

'They are going to be married?' Nicky felt a chill run over her skin as they climbed into the upper floors. The stone walls must be damp, she told herself. Why else should she begin to tremble with an aching coldness?

CHAPTER FIVE

THE room which had been made ready for Paul was enormous. His cot, clearly bought specially for him, was painted white and embossed with colourful drawings of animals. The bedclothes were all exquisite—the quilt white hand-sewn with gay flowers, the sheets a delicate lavender. Beside it stood a toy cupboard. Shelves above it held pretty picture books, a clown puppet and some games. An adult bed took up the other half of the room.

'I shall sleep there,' Nicola indicated politely.

Angelina looked mutinous. 'It is not as the order was given,' she mumbled.

'I am Paul's mother—I shall sleep in his room, as I have always done until now. It would be a mistake to change too many things at once. When he is used to this place I may move out of the room, but for the moment it is wisest to make him feel as secure as possible.'

Angelina listened with a doubtful air. She shrugged. 'As you wish, *signora*.' There was a grudging respect in the tones, however, and Nicola could see that the other woman's attitude to her had altered since their first clash downstairs. The discovery that she could speak

Italian had made Angelina rather more inclined to like her, Nicola suspected. It made her less of a foreign intruder, presumably.

Paul sagged weakly on to the bed, his head lolling. Nicola began to undress him, and Angelina gestured to the wash basin on the far side of the room. Paul wriggled as his mother washed his face and hands. His yawns were wider now and he could hardly keep his eyes open.

Nicola tumbled him gently into his cot. In his pyjamas, his dark hair slightly damp and curly on his forehead, his eyelids lowered over the bright black eyes, he looked more of a baby than ever.

Angelina knelt beside the cot and gazed at him through the bars, her face engrossed. Tenderness lit the sallow skin, gave lustre to the eyes.

'He is his father's child! So beautiful! An angel!'

Nicola smiled, amused and touched. 'He looks angelic now, yes,' she agreed wryly. 'But you'll have a hard job keeping up with him once he's wide awake.'

Angelina laughed eagerly. '*Signora*,' she said, in a husky voice, 'you will permit that I look after him? You will not keep him all to yourself?'

Nicola was both ashamed and moved. 'I shall be very grateful for your help, Angelina,' she said quickly. She had not wanted to hurt the other woman.

'His father was like my own child,' Angelina explained humbly. 'I was happy to tend him, to hold him in my arms. It will be a joy to do so with this little one, a joy I had not believed possible.' She looked up at Nicola, her lips trembling. 'I hated you, *signora*—see, I admit it freely. I believed you wicked for stealing our Paolo from us. But that is past. You bring me another Paolo, so I am in your debt now. You will forgive me for the hatred?'

'Of course,' Nicola assured her gravely. 'I do understand, you know. I see how you must have felt.'

Angelina's gratitude made her face softer, more youthful. She looked once more at Paul. He was fast asleep, his thumb in his mouth, his cheeks flushed.

'He sleeps, the small one. Will you permit that I show you the room we made ready? We could move the cot into that room tomorrow.'

'This room will suit me very well,' Nicola assured her. 'Tell me, who else lives here, besides Bianca and Signor Lorenzo?'

'There is Domenico,' said Angelina. 'He lives here, too—and his mother, of course.'

'Signora Farenze was not there when we arrived?'

'She rarely leaves her room until the evening. She is very delicate.'

'I understood she was in charge of the household?'

Angelina nodded. 'But of course—she gives the orders. Bianca is too young.'

'When will I meet Signora Farenze?'

Angelina shrugged. 'She asked that you be brought to see her as soon as you had rested after your journey. If I turn down the covers on this bed will you rest?' She moved to the window and let down the blind. A cool shadow made the room peaceful. Nicola looked longingly at the bed.

'It would be pleasant,' she admitted.

Angelina gestured to her to sit on the bed. Kneeling, she removed her shoes. 'I will call you an hour before dinner. You may then bathe and change—tonight the Signor Lorenzo changes for dinner in your honour. But now—sleep if you can.'

To Nicola's astonishment she slid into a light sleep immediately on closing her eyes. Her weary body relaxed. The coolness of the room brought rest and refreshment. She awoke at six when Paul began to stir, his long sleep leaving him hungry and curious about this new home.

'I want my tea,' he demanded as she smiled at him. 'Why are you in bed, Mummy? Is it morning?'

'It's evening,' she said, laughing. 'You slept for a long time. Stay there and I'll see what I can find.'

She went to the door and peered out. A narrow corridor wound on either side of the room. She vaguely recalled having come from the left, and moved towards it to look for the staircase.

A door opened. Domenico came out and stood still, staring at her, his brows arched in amusement. 'Barefoot?'

She flushed, looking down at her toes in surprise. She had forgotten to put her shoes on when Paul called her.

'I was looking for Angelina. Paul is hungry.'

He opened the door behind him once more and gestured. 'Kill two birds with one stone—come in and meet my mother and ring Angelina at the same time.'

'Ring her?' Sleep had apparently made her stupid because she did not seem to understand him quickly enough.

'There is a house telephone system. There is a phone in your room. You merely dial the kitchen and speak to Angelina. A house this size needs some sort of communication. We couldn't shout, could we?'

She flushed again, thinking that he was a supercilious beast. How should she have known about this telephone system? She had not been told about it. There was no need for him to drawl with such mockery.

The room into which he ushered her was luxurious without being over-ornate. The ceiling, high and covered with stucco cherubs, was somewhat muted by the delicacy of the curtains and carpet—a gentle pastel green. The bedclothes matched, and on the green pillows lay a frail, lined face, the eyes almost astonishingly alive as they smiled across the room at Nicola.

'Welcome to the Villa Farenze, my dear,' said a soft Italian voice.

Nicola smiled back. Domenico's mother had fine silver hair, brushed loose about her face; eyes of the same colour as her son, and a mouth of great tenderness and spirit.

She did not look Italian, Nicola thought vaguely. 'What a lovely room you have,' she murmured politely.

Signora Farenze laughed softly. 'Yes. I like to have a great deal of green around me. It reminds me of England.'

'England?' Nicola's voice rose in surprise.

The old lady looked at her son in inquiry. 'But you have not told her? Why not, Nico?'

He looked sardonically at Nicola. 'She was so violently anti-Italian that I thought it might sound like an apology if I told her I was half English myself.'

Nicola threw him a cold glance, then turned back to his mother. 'You're English?'

'I was born there,' smiled the Signora. 'But my family lived here in Italy for so long that I am really more than half Italian myself. Italian is my tongue, although of course I speak English, and I do love to be in England in the spring.' She sighed, her eyes seeking a print of a Constable landscape which hung opposite her bed. 'I shall never go there again now. I must live on my memories.'

'Which part of England did you come from?' asked Nicola.

'Norfolk was where my relatives lived. That was where I stayed when I went to England for a holiday each year—always in the spring. So green and new. Everything seemed freshly born each morning.' Her eyes rose to seek the blue Italian sky outside her window. Dusk was softly veiling it now, a melancholy, romantic deepening of the colour. Nicola saw that Signora Farenze in fact had blue eyes, a pale blue which was several shades brighter than the grey eyes she had handed on to her son.

Looking back at her again, the Signora laughed. 'But I chose Italy, and it is Italy which holds my happiest memories of life. I would not be happy anywhere else. Divided loyalties are always the most painful.'

Nicola nodded. 'Yes, I think you're right.' She thought of her son and winced. A terrible choice awaited both of them.

Signora Farenze noted her expression and sighed sympathetically. 'Yes, you too know the pain of choice!'

Domenico had moved closer. Nicola could feel him just behind her shoulder. 'She married an Italian,' he said harshly. 'When she did so she made her choice. A wife must belong to the land of her husband—the Bible tells us so.'

His mother frowned and looked surprised. 'Nico! You speak with unkindness to Nicola.' She smiled at the girl. 'You permit me to call you that? You will call me Aunt Francesca?'

'Thank you. I would like to.'

Domenico moved to the bedside table and picked up the telephone. He spoke crisply, in Italian, then replaced the receiver. 'Angelina will bring Paul some tea at once. She asked what he would like—I told her to bring a boiled egg and some bread and butter. That will suit, I imagine?'

'Perfectly,' she said stiffly.

'When shall I have the happiness of seeing him?' Aunt Francesca asked eagerly.

'Shall I bring him to see you now? He is awake.'

'Would you do that for me? That would make me so glad.'

Nicola hurried back to the room she shared with Paul. He was sitting up in his cot staring at the toys on the shelves. 'Are they for me?' He spoke in a hushed voice. 'Or is there another boy here?'

'I think they're for you,' she told him.

'Can I play with them now, Mummy?'

'Later, dear. I want you to come and meet a new auntie—you must call her Aunt Francesca. She's very old, so you'll be good, won't you, Paul?'

'Yes, Mummy,' he promised. 'Mummy, are there lots of people in this family?'

'I think there are quite a few people,' she agreed.

He sighed. 'Are they all old, every single one? No children at all?'

She laughed. 'We'll have to ask Aunt Francesca about that, dear. Come along and see her.' She lifted him up and carried him along the corridor to the other room.

Domenico was seated beside the bed. He looked sardonically at her bare feet and she wished angrily that he would stop teasing. She wished, too, that she had remembered to put on her shoes. She was so used to running about barefoot in the flat in London that she found it hard to remember that here things were not quite so informal.

Signora Farenze was charmed by Paul, and made him sit on the bed beside her and talk to her. He asked her about other children, and she said sadly that there were very few in the family, but that there were distant cousins who had children of his age and older.

'We must invite them here to play with you,' she promised.

Angelina came in a moment later and took Paul back to his own room for his tea. Nicola softly slipped away, too, and found that Angelina had already run a bath for her. Fluffy white towels hung on the towel rail. Jars and bottles of deliciously scented things stood on a glass shelf high above the wash basin. The water was delicately fragrant and Nicola slid into it with gratitude, feeling her tired muscles relax.

When she returned to her room she found Paul back in his cot. Angelina was singing to him in liquid Italian, her dark face intent. He was yawning as Nicola kissed him goodnight. Long before she had finished dressing he was fast asleep once more.

They dined at eight, she had discovered from Aunt Francesca. Domenico took her down to a cool, shuttered salon on the courtyard side of the house. The floor was of ancient blue-white marble, veined and polished by many feet. Candles flared, smoking a little, in the breeze which blew in from the courtyard through open glass doors. The curtains hanging beside them moved swishingly, blowing back into the room.

The scent of geraniums, heady and drowsy, wafted across the room. She could see them, massed in a stone trough outside, their vivid scarlet and salmon pink making a bold splash of colour against the growing darkness.

Somewhere, not too far away, someone played a guitar. The notes plucked gently at the silence. The tune was unfamiliar, but Nicola found it nostalgic and insidious, a haunting melody full of love and yearning.

She ate veal in a rich wine sauce, and pasta, and drank wine made from grapes grown in the family vineyards.

Vanessa talked, laughed, gestured. A golden halo seemed to glitter around her Botticelli head as she smiled intimately at Domenico. He was attentive, bending towards her to smile, murmuring, raising his glass in a silent toast.

Bianca sat opposite them, glowering. She picked at her food, pushing it around on her plate as a child might do, her lower lip caught between her small, white teeth. Oddly, for all her hostility and rudeness, Nicola was suddenly reminded of a child—a naughty, hurt, defiant child.

Lorenzo Farenze sat at the head of the table, his leonine head lowered as though he were about to charge. He wore a black dinner jacket, plain white evening shirt, and black tie.

Vanessa had spent a long time in choosing the perfect evening dress for her first dinner at the Villa. She had rejected several before finally deciding on a classical gown of champagne silk, uncluttered and elegant, which left her throat and shoulders bare and emphasised her delicately feline look.

Nicola had only packed two dresses suitable for even-

87

ing wear. She had chosen a flower-printed chiffon for tonight. It was pale green and had the shadows of yellow flowers drifting over its folds. She had allowed Vanessa to comb her hair up into a french roll, but had decided when she saw herself in the mirror that it gave her rather a severe appearance.

Domenico passed her the fruit bowl, his grey eyes assessing her with a cool flick of the lids. 'I prefer your hair down,' he said calmly. 'It does not suit you like that—you look like a schoolteacher.'

'Oh?' She chose something from the bowl without even seeing what she held.

Bianca said maliciously, 'We expected you to look like a street-walker!'

'Bianca!' Lorenzo's voice struck her like a whip. 'Have you lost all manners? How dare you speak so to a guest!'

'I am not a hypocrite, that is all!' she spat back, tossing her black head defiantly.

'You behave like a gutter urchin,' he said menacingly. 'I will not tolerate it in my house. You mend your manners or you go.'

'You would turn me out for her?' Bianca was aghast and white.

'You offend a guest at my table,' he said sternly. 'You must be punished for it.'

'Where would I go?' Her eyes were like wet black stones as she stared at him.

'Your brother has room enough in his house. Either you watch your tongue or you go to Leo.'

'What's all this about me?' The voice drawled from the doorway into the courtyard and all eyes turned towards it.

The man who stood there was curly-headed, dark and broad, with a handsome face full of wicked amusement. He held a guitar in one hand, the brightly coloured strap hanging. His silk shirt was orange, his tight pants black. He looked for all the world like a Spanish flamenco dancer, thought Nicky with relish. She glanced at Domenico and found him watching her closely.

The grey eyes were narrowed, the face grim. She looked away from him, suppressing a smile. She remembered his warnings about Leo's attitude to women. Certainly, she thought, Leo was obviously very attractive to the opposite sex. His stance as he lounged against the wall told her that. He expected to arouse their interest.

'Come in, Leo,' said Lorenzo in a resigned voice.

'Why wasn't I invited to this distinguished gathering, or need I ask?' Leo strolled into the room. 'You've finished your meal, I see. Am I too humble to join you for coffee?'

'I did not invite you because I wanted to keep the party small for this first evening,' Lorenzo said sharply.

Leo's bright, impudent gaze skimmed their faces. He grinned at his sister, swiftly inspected Vanessa and then Nicola.

'Paolo wrote to us that Nicola had hair like black silk,' he said flippantly. 'So I suppose I may guess which is the mother of our little Principino!'

She gave him a long, thoughtful look as he stared at her. 'Yes, I'm Nicola.'

The insolent eyes surveyed every visible inch of her, at leisure and with some appreciation. 'Paolo had good taste,' he commented at last.

Domenico's hand stiffened where it lay on the table. Nicola, looking away from Leo's gaze, saw the long fingers curl into a fist, the knuckles show white.

'Sit down, Leo,' Domenico said icily.

Leo drew up a chair and sat down between his mother and sister. He grinned at Domenico. 'Do I feel a rapier at my ribs? I wonder why.'

'Nico probably feels as I do, that you need a lesson in good manners,' snapped Vanessa.

Nicola blinked in astonishment. She had never heard her sister speak so sharply to an attractive man before. It was incomprehensible. Had Vanessa taken an instant dislike to Leo? Or was it merely that she was siding with Domenico against the newcomer? A newcomer, of course, who had apparently been unimpressed by Vanessa's golden beauty, a fact which, in itself, was enough to make her detest him.

Leo was looking at Vanessa now, though, his eyebrows raised in mute astonishment and wry mockery. Vanessa flushed under his gaze. Leo laughed softly as she looked away.

'Are you going to teach me manners, *signorina*?' His drawl was charged with taunting amusement. 'Nico, introduce us!'

'Vanessa knows who you are, Leo,' snapped Domenico. 'She is Nicola's sister, Vanessa Mayfield.'

'A charming name,' Leo murmured. 'Two such beautiful girls! Yet so unalike! Yours was a lucky family. Are there more of you in England?'

'No,' Nicola told him, since it was plain that Vanessa would not speak. 'We are the only two left.'

'And you are both to live here at the Villa?'

Lorenzo exerted himself once more. 'Leo, you will drink your coffee and be silent. I have told you what I think of your manners before. You will lead your wild life in your tower—here I expect at least lip service to my ideals.'

'Dear Uncle Lorenzo,' he murmured, tongue in cheek.

Bianca stirred uneasily, her dark eyes seeking those of her brother. Nicola saw that she appealed to him to placate Lorenzo Farenze, and that Leo first shrugged, then smiled reassurance. Clearly, despite his flippancy, Leo had affection for one member at least of this household.

'You paint, I understand?' she asked politely, in an effort to lead the conversation into safer topics.

'In a fashion,' Leo nodded, his expression changing.

'Do not permit him to lure either of you into his tower on a pretence of painting you,' Domenico said sharply. 'His paintings are unrecognisable as people. They have no limbs or features—they are mere wraiths of shapes, splodges of pale paint.'

'My cousin the art critic,' Leo drawled.

'I am not ignorant of art,' Domenico said. 'You are a typical dilettante, Leo. Art, for you, is an excuse for idleness.'

Leo's eyes narrowed. 'I bow to your superior knowledge, cousin.' The sarcasm was charged with hostility.

'Idleness which affords you time for your real occupation,' Domenico went on bitingly.

'And what is that?' Leo asked, his lip curling with hauteur.

'Flirtation, amusing yourself by playing with the emotions of silly young girls!' Domenico stared at him with icy implacability. 'You are a menace, Leo. You turn their heads and break their hearts, and it is left to us to placate their families and smooth down furious fathers.'

Leo leaned back, fiddling with the spoon in his saucer, his dark eyes narrow and half veiled by drooped lids. 'You make me sound like Don Juan, cousin. I hope that the two newcomers in our midst realise that this tirade from Nico is a warning specifically delivered for their benefit?' He let his lids rise. His eyes trailed over Vanessa, rested on Nicola. 'Do you feel yourself in danger from my charm, *signora*? If so—heed Nico and beware!'

She smiled, slightly embarrassed. 'I doubt if I am in any danger, but thank you for the warning.'

Leo's eyes widened and were fixed on hers for a second or two. His smile deepened and became more genuine. The deliberate impudence left his face. He rose, bent across the table, lifted her hand and kissed her fingers with dramatic gallantry.

'Nicola,' he murmured. 'An enchanting name ...'

She laughed. 'I think you're a fraud,' she said lightly.

He looked at her in inquiry. 'Is that kind?'

'You like playing games,' she nodded quizzically. 'And you are always surprised to find that other people don't understand your rules!'

He laughed out loud. 'Beautiful and clever—a combination not often met with in this drab world! I salute the memory of Paolo—he found a perfect jewel. Nicola, you and I shall be friends, yes?'

She let his eyes hold hers, saw sincerity beneath the flaunted impudence, and felt a curious liking and sympathy for him. 'Yes,' she said quietly, 'we shall be friends, I think.'

Domenico's chair scraped across the marble floor. 'Shall we remove to the courtyard for an hour, Lorenzo?' His voice was icy with restraint.

CHAPTER SIX

WHEN Nicola woke up next morning she was at first bewildered to find herself in a strange room, but a few seconds later she was sitting bolt up, smiling at Paul, who had climbed out of his cot and wandered across to sit on her chest with a thump expressive of affection and hunger.

'Want breakfast,' he mumbled, choking her with a hug around her neck.

She kissed his nose. 'You shall have it, my pet. Let Mummy get up and she'll help you dress.'

The door opened and Angelina glided into the room, bearing a tray, her sallow face wreathed in smiles. Paul recognised her vaguely and gave her a congratulatory beam, seeing the food she carried. Someone who anticipated his wants in this fashion must be encouraged.

Delighted, Angelina laid the tray down. *'Buon giorno, Paolo!'*

Paul scrambled down from the bed and toddled over to her. 'My breakfast?'

He scanned the contents of the tray. Fruit juice, boiled eggs, coffee and hot rolls. 'Pop and squeak,' he said crossly.

Angelina was bewildered. 'What does he say?' she appealed to Nicola, who laughed.

'He wants the cereal he has at home. Paul, for today just eat an egg.'

'Negg,' he agreed amiably. He looked around, waiting for the usual ritual to commence. 'Bib?'

Angelina hurried to produce one from the drawers in which she had bestowed their clothes last night. Paul patiently waited while she tied the bib around him.

'Negg,' he murmured, picking up his spoon. Angelina split and buttered a roll for him, and he looked at it in consternation. 'Soldiers?'

Angelina was aghast. 'Soldiers? How is that?'

His mother interpreted once more. 'He likes to have sliced bread and butter cut into fingers, thin pieces. He calls them soldiers.' She patted Paul's rosy cheek. 'The roll is delicious, darling. Don't be so conservative.'

He frowned, then accepted the roll. Silence fell, a contented silence, during which Paul ate and the two women watched him with fascination.

'I look after him for you, *signora*,' Angelina offered eagerly. 'You are to go for a ride in the car with the Signor.'

'The old Signor—or Domenico?' Nicola hesitated.

'The old Signor—Signor Lorenzo himself.'

Paul looked up, interested, spoon in hand. 'The lion, my grandfather,' he said thickly through his mouthful of food.

'Don't speak with your mouth full, my darling,'

Nicola said absently, but with a smile. 'Do you know where we're going, Angelina?' she went on.

'To visit the vineyards this morning, and then to drive down into Florence,' said Angelina.

Nicola said thoughtfully, 'That should be very interesting. Are you sure Paul won't be too much trouble?'

Angelina's laughter was convincing. 'It will make me very happy to look after him! Will he stay with me, do you think? He will not be shy with Angelina?'

'He is used to being left with babysitters,' said Nicola. 'Once he gets to know you, and to feel at home here in the Villa, he'll be quite happy. Paul is a well-adjusted little boy.'

'He is an angel,' the other woman nodded vigorously.

Paul had finished his breakfast. He drained his cup of milky coffee and set it down with a bang, wiping his mouth on his bib.

Angelina bore him off to the bathroom while Nicola looked through her wardrobe for suitable clothes. She chose a white linen dress and a broad-brimmed hat. They were simple enough for everyday wear, yet elegant enough for a visit to Florence.

When she had seen Paul dressed she departed for the bathroom herself. When she descended, dressed and ready for the morning, she found Paul playing on a small tricycle in the courtyard while Angelina watched him, a basket of vegetables in her lap which she was busily preparing for lunch. Her plump hands moved deftly while she kept her dark eyes on Paul.

Nicola watched them both for a moment before she

stepped out to speak to them. Paul greeted her enthusiastically, waving one small hand as he cycled.

'Mummy, see me—I've got a bike!'

'It belonged to one of my cousin's children,' Angelina explained with a smile. 'He is too big for it now.'

'Paul is in heaven, isn't he?' Nicola watched her son with pleasure. It was wonderful to see him so happy. 'Thank you very much, Angelina. I'm grateful. Paul has always wanted to be able to ride about freely. Life in a London flat can be restricting for a small child.'

'I am glad you are honest enough to admit so much!' The voice behind her made her start and turn, her cheeks pink.

Domenico eyed her quizzically. 'I did not think you would ever admit that it might be good for Paul to live here!'

'Having money and freedom may be pleasant, but they are not always the wisest choice for one's children,' she said quietly.

He stared at Paul, circling cheerfully, making a hooting noise as he turned. 'The child looks happy. What is wrong with that, my puritan?'

'Nothing,' she said flatly. Angelina looked from one to the other of them blankly, puzzled by the very obvious tension which stretched between them.

'Lorenzo wants to take you to the vineyards today. Then he has booked a table for lunch at his favourite restaurant in Florence—it's small and dark and serves the best food in Italy.'

She looked at Paul. 'Angelina mentioned it earlier.

She's going to watch Paul for me.'

'And you agreed?' His tone mocked her. 'Wonders will never cease!'

'You have totally the wrong impression of my attitude to Paul,' she said crossly. 'I wanted to be around until he got used to the new surroundings, but now he's beginning to feel at home here I see no reason why I shouldn't leave him in capable hands for a while.'

'How did you manage while you were at work? Did your sister look after him?'

'Sometimes,' she admitted. 'Our other flatmate was very kind, too. I managed somehow.'

He looked at her through narrowed eyes. 'Yes, you are very capable, aren't you?'

The word made her sound unfeminine and dull. She turned her head away to hide her chagrin. A loose strand of shining hair fell along the line of her cheek and she idly tucked it back behind her ear until she could get to a mirror to rearrange her hair style in its smooth chignon.

Vanessa erupted into the courtyard, slender and angelic in a modern imitation of peasant costume—a white broderie anglaise blouse with puff sleeves threaded with pale blue ribbon, full swirling skirt of crisp floral cotton tied at the waist with a wide sash of blue satin. She looked like a little girl, her gold curls bouncing, her eyes bright and interested.

Nicola felt a little shiver of alarm, though, as she met Vanessa's vivid blue stare, and saw the thinly veiled rage which her sister permitted to show briefly. Vanessa was angry, yes. But why?

'How long have you two been down?' Vanessa spoke lightly, but Nicola was suddenly enlightened. Vanessa suspected her of having stolen a march by getting up early. The pursuit of Domenico was serious enough for Vanessa to resent any lost moment of time with him.

She moved back into the house, leaving Vanessa with him, and found Lorenzo drinking black coffee in a sunny morning room, every inch of which was crammed with plants, leaving only a couple of wicker chairs and a wicker table free.

Lorenzo smiled at her. This morning he looked fragile and worn. The excitement of the day before had clearly left him tired. His skin seemed more yellow than ever, his eyes embedded in folded wrinkles. Despite this, his expression was one of deep happiness, and Nicola felt that Paul's arrival had given him a joy he had imagined lost to him for ever.

'You know my plans for today? You approve them, *mia cara*?' He spoke to her with a voice so gentle, so deep and mild. She looked back, with astonishment, at her image of him—the image his son, her husband, had created in her mind. The two pictures did not coincide at any point. This kind and serious man was not the domineering, autocratic father Paolo had described. Had she misunderstood, or had Paolo seen another side of him?

'I am looking forward to seeing the vineyards,' she agreed. 'Are you sure it will not tire you?'

He shook his head. 'I shall enjoy showing them to you. Nicola, we have much to say to each other. Domenico will drive us. If your sister sits with him in the front of the car, you can sit beside me in the back and listen to what I have to tell you. Will you do this?'

'Of course, Signor Lorenzo.'

He took her hand between both of his and gazed at her gravely. 'Can you not call me Pappa?'

She hesitated, flushing, and he sighed.

'Well, we will not hurry. *Festina lente . . .*' He looked up, a trifle quizzically at her face. 'Do you understand that?'

She shook her head, smiling.

'It means make haste slowly—it is Latin, an old Latin tag which we use. Old age brings an appreciation of time which the young would not understand, *cara*. The hours speed by. We long to slow them down, to cling to their tails and make them pass like snails instead of racehorses.'

'Paul will help you with that,' she said gently. 'Children do seem to make time pass more slowly.'

He stood up, courtly and gallant in his immaculate linen and exquisitely cut suit. 'Children and beautiful women,' he agreed, taking her hand.

A sleek limousine took them to the vineyards. As Signor Farenze wished, Nicola sat in the back with him while Domenico drove with Vanessa beside him. The windows were wound right down so that a stream of fresh, sweet air flowed around them. They passed olive groves, pastures full of cypress and goats grazing on

100

rough, rocky hillocks and the endless vineyards, green with the new life at the moment.

'How sweet the air is here,' Nicola sighed, breathing deeply. 'It seems to be fragrant.'

'Fragrant? Yes, yes, the air of the hills is sweet as honey, as strong as wine.' Signor Farenze sounded vague, though he spoke clearly and intelligibly enough. His eyes were fixed on her face, a frown on his lined forehead.

She looked back, waiting for him to go on with whatever it was he had wanted to say to her. After a moment of silence, he said softly, '*Cara*, I know how you have felt about me. I have been a blind, foolish old man, and it would have been mere justice if you had denied me my grandson. When I heard of the marriage, I was so angry that I had a stroke. They told you?'

'Domenico told me, yes.'

'And you no doubt thought it was the hand of God!'

'Oh, no,' she said, shocked.

He shrugged his shoulders, lifting his hands in a Latin gesture of wry acceptance. 'But yes, I believe it was, in a way. I was brought to see that I did not own my son, that nothing in life is for ever. We all have our possessions on a short lease from God. Our own bodies, our own minds, are only a loan from the eternal. I learnt late, and in a hard fashion—but I think I learnt well. When Domenico telephoned to tell me that I had a grandson living I was quite out of my head with joy. Angelina feared for my life, I think.'

101

Nicola touched his hand. 'I am glad you weathered it!'

He laughed. 'Once the shock passed I was so eager to see the boy that I would have turned away death's angel from my door with my own hands! For this, *cara*, this is my chance of redemption—this boy is sent to me for a reason.'

She looked at him uneasily. What did he mean? Surely Domenico had told him that she did not mean to stay here in Italy for ever?

He saw her expression. The dark eyes stayed on her face, trying to read her thoughts. 'You will not take him away from me now? I am not long for this world. I shall not have much time with him.'

'I . . .' Nicola's voice failed her. She saw Domenico's head turn slightly, knew that he had been listening intently to what the old man said, that he, too, was waiting for her to answer.

Vanessa spoke before she had had a chance to gather her thoughts, to phrase her reply gently.

'Of course we will stay, *signore*. Where else should Paul be but with his grandfather, in his father's old home? Paolo spoke about the Villa so often! He loved it so much. He would have wanted his son to grow up here.'

Lorenzo leaned back against the cushions with a long, hard sigh Domenico looked at Nicola, in the driving mirror, and she saw the tautness of his tanned features. He knew very well that Vanessa did not speak

102

for her. Lorenzo might be fooled, but Domenico was not.

'You forgive me, *cara*?' The whisper made her start, and she turned to smile at him.

'Yes, I forgive you.'

'We made a bad start, you and I. Now we shall begin again, for Paolo's sake.'

She nodded. 'Yes, for his sake.'

'I wish I had known of his death earlier. It grieves me that there was no one from his family at his funeral. They did not tell me because I was so ill, but they should have done. Death cancels all debts.'

'Someone wrote to me,' Nicola said slowly. 'Who was that?'

He looked thoughtful. 'Was it your mother, Domenico?'

Domenico shook his head. 'No, nor was it myself. I do not know who wrote. What did the letter say?'

Nicola did not answer for a moment. 'It doesn't matter,' she said at last. 'I forget exactly . . .'

Domenico eyed her curiously in the mirror. 'You mentioned this before. I must find out who wrote. Who was in the house? Bianca?'

Lorenzo looked astonished. 'Bianca would not have written on my behalf, surely.'

'She might have written on her own behalf,' Domenico said with a flat intonation.

Lorenzo clicked his tongue. 'So? This letter was . . . not a kind one?' He looked at Nicola anxiously.

'Not very kind,' she said grudgingly, wishing she had never asked. 'It doesn't matter. The past is past.'

'I must ask Bianca about this,' Lorenzo said sternly.

'Please! I thought we had agreed that we should have a general amnesty about the whole past? Isn't Bianca to be given the same chance?'

Lorenzo smiled reluctantly. 'You are generous, *cara*.'

Vanessa turned to look at Nicola, her eyebrows arched in irritation. 'Oh, she's very generous,' she said sweetly, but her eyes darted angrily at her sister. 'I hope you aren't making a mistake about Bianca, though, Nicky. I'm very much afraid she detests you.'

Lorenzo frowned. 'That is not good news. How dare that chit set herself up against me?' The autocrat was not buried, it seemed, merely dormant.

The car swung, at that moment, into a narrow drive, and the subject was abandoned, to Nicola's relief. They had arrived at the Farenze vineyards.

Lorenzo insisted on showing them round himself, although Domenico offered his services. Leaning heavily on a stick, his leonine head defiantly raised to sniff the air, the old man walked beside Nicola between the vines. When they reached the house once more he was exhausted, pale and breathing heavily, and Domenico eyed him angrily.

'You have overdone it, Lorenzo!'

'Is she to see the vineyard with anyone but me?' The deep voice was stiff with pride. 'It was my duty, my honour. She is the mother of the next Lion. I shall not see the child reach his majority—and Nicola must

104

watch over his inheritance during the years between. I wanted her to know as much as possible.'

Domenico was tight-lipped, narrow-eyed. 'You did not trust me in this, Lorenzo?'

The old man looked at him with compunction. 'I do not want to offend you, Domenico! It was not a matter of trust. It was the desire of my heart ...'

'You will put a woman in charge here?' Domenico asked him coolly. 'How could that be?'

'She is my grandson's mother! Who has a better right? Who has more of an interest in seeing the business thrive?'

'But a woman, Lorenzo?' Domenico's voice was hard. 'How could she make decisions, plan ahead, manage the staff?'

'I am not talking of the everyday running of affairs,' the old man said with an irritable gesture. 'That will still stay in your hands, of course, Domenico.'

'Then what did you mean?' Domenico's face was cold. Nicola opened her mouth to protest that she wanted no part in the business, but Vanessa gripped her arm tightly, her nails digging into her sister's flesh, and surprise held her silent. She looked at Vanessa. The blue eyes were bright, and fixed on the two men. What was Vanessa up to? Nicola thought.

Lorenzo was speaking again, his voice arrogantly offhand. 'You will be responsible to Nicola, of course. You will answer to her for what you do.'

Domenico's features were suddenly rigid. Nicola

105

saw his grey eyes freeze over, his mouth tighten into a thin, angry line.

'You expect me to be answerable to a woman? A woman ignorant of the special problems of this business? A foreigner who knows nothing of Italy, of labour problems, of export and import?' The words stung like ice-tipped darts, and Nicola flushed bitterly.

'What makes you think I want any of this?' Despite her sister's attempt again to silence her, she burst out into stammered anger. 'You've both been talking about me as if I was invisible! Why didn't you ask me? I would have made this ludicrous argument unnecessary, since I have no intention of accepting these plans for my future. What my son does when he is of age is another matter. I shall not stay here to run the Farenze business, or interfere with the rest of the family in their running of it.'

Lorenzo looked with bitter anguish at Domenico. 'See what you have done! You will drive her away from Farenze! Or is that your desire, Domenico Farenze?'

Domenico seized Nicola by the elbow and propelled her away from the rest of the party, pushing her lagging feet along by sheer brute force, half carrying her. He stopped when they had reached a silent corner of the green vineyard. His hand dropped from her elbow. Resentfully, she rubbed the red mark he had left on her flesh.

'Must you always behave like a caveman?' she demanded.

He stared, then laughed, yet still angrily, his grey eyes sparkling. 'You think me too impulsive? That is odd. I would have said the same of you.'

'What must the others think? We can't just rush off like this!'

He thrust his hands into the depths of his pockets in a most uncharacteristic gesture and rocked to and fro on his heels. 'I had things to say to you which would not bear an audience.'

'Oh?' She was alarmed and uneasy.

'You will not hurt Lorenzo, Nicola—do you hear?' His voice was abrupt, intimate. 'He is not long for this world.'

The finality made her blink up at him. 'Are you certain of that, Domenico?'

'His doctor assures me of it,' he said sombrely. He turned and stared at the green vines. She watched him, thinking how magnificently he dominated his surroundings, his dark head arrogantly tilted, the straight nose and powerful jawline giving him a strength which the commanding grey eyes emphasised.

Quietly, she said, 'You began the argument, though. I do not want him to leave me control of the Farenze estate. I would prefer it to remain in your hands.'

He shrugged. 'Lorenzo would not have been hurt by that, my dear girl. He understands a male reluctance to work under a woman. The discussion would have been resolved amicably.'

'How?' she asked in disbelief.

'By a compromise, of course.' His grey eyes taunted

107

her. 'Something of which you are totally ignorant. You flew off in a tantrum without waiting to see how we would resolve the problem.'

Nicola ignored his teasing. 'What compromise?'

'I imagine Lorenzo would have agreed to a joint trusteeship, with both you and me working in harmony.' His mouth curled mockingly. 'Harmony of a sort!'

She turned away to pluck a green leaf, her cheeks flushed. 'Oh! I see!'

'Would that be acceptable to you, too?'

She hesitated. 'It would mean that I must stay here in Italy, of course.'

'Of course,' he said.

She felt a strange reluctance to give a definite answer. 'I don't know ...'

'Think about it,' he advised her. 'I will speak to Lorenzo. We will leave the situation for the present. Time will resolve it, no doubt.'

They walked slowly back through the green valleys of vines. A gentle shadow lay over them. The sun had climbed high overhead and the distant hills shimmered with a blue haze which was fast vanishing in the noontide heat.

Domenico paused to look down at her. Forced to stop, too, she flushed slightly as she met his grey gaze.

'What was it like to be in love with Paolo?' There was a cynical twist to his lips as he asked the question.

Astonished, she stammered, 'What a strange thing to ask!'

'Is it? But it must have been a strange affair, Paolo and a shy young English girl! You are nothing like the girl of whom he wrote to me— I had a certain picture of you, dark hair and bright green eyes, dazzlingly lovely!' He spoke in an odd tone, half lazily, half angrily.

'You still resent me,' she said on a sigh.

'I? Why should I resent you?' He looked searchingly at her.

'Don't you? Everyone else did, and I think both you and Bianca still do!'

'You are wrong,' he said flatly. 'You cannot understand my feelings. And I think you are attempting to evade my question. When you think about Paolo what do you feel?' There was an urgency about the question which puzzled her.

She shrugged. 'Strangely enough I think I have a hazier idea of him now than I did in England. Coming to Italy has changed me somehow.' She frowned. 'I think it has shaken the kaleidoscope, altered the pattern. Paolo seems a different person against this background.'

'How different?' he asked her sharply.

'The things he told me about his family ...' She broke off, feeling a disloyalty to her dead husband in this discussion. 'No!' She turned away. 'Let's drop the matter, shall we?'

Lorenzo looked at her hopefully when she joined him again. 'Has Domenico soothed you, *mia cara*?'

Domenico grinned lazily at him. 'I think the ruffled

109

feathers are smoothed down again, Lorenzo! All women need to be stroked.'

Nicola glared at him, chin up. 'How unwise of you to expose your tactics to me, Domenico! I will anticipate your moves in future.'

Lorenzo chuckled delightedly. 'Ah, I envy you, Nico —to be young, to enjoy the battle of the sexes! And with such a lovely creature as Nicola ...'

Vanessa, listening with narrowed eyes, looked at her sister in a frozen silence. Nicola, meeting that look, was alarmed. Vanessa was quite capable of mischief if she felt herself threatened, and she had already made her interest in Domenico only too clear.

CHAPTER SEVEN

THEIR first visit to Florence was so exciting that Nicola still had the dreams in her eyes when they arrived back at the Villa. Leo, lounging in the courtyard with his inevitable guitar, greeted her with a smile of curiosity.

'You look like a girl in a trance!'

'I feel like one. I've just been to Florence.'

'Ah!' His eyes shone with deep pleasure. 'Florence is one of the seven wonders of the world. A city of giants.'

'Giants?' She was bewildered briefly.

'Artistic giants,' he explained. 'All of the great Renaissance artists came here—the city is crammed with beauty, choked with it. What impressed you most?'

'The Medici tombs,' she said, with a shiver. 'The atmosphere in there—a brooding power, ice cold and menacing! I've never felt anything like it!'

Leo grimaced. 'Is that what you will take back to England with you as your chief memory of Florence? The menace of the Medici chapels? What about Michelangelo's David? The Perseus? What about ...'

'What about allowing Nicola to take a peaceful

siesta?' Vanessa's drawl was insulting and Leo shot her a furious look.

'Does art bore you, my beautiful?' His dark eyes flicked her contemptuously. 'Never mind—we can't have brains and beauty, can we?'

'Am I supposed to feel insulted?' Vanessa purred at him. 'Sorry, but I don't! Most artists are just spongers who use their art as an excuse for getting out of doing any work. Nice work if you can get it—but don't expect to be admired for it as well.'

Leo strummed negligently, his handsome face an insolent mask. Over the music he murmured, 'How is the fishing coming along?'

Vanessa was taken off guard. 'Fishing?' She looked at him in puzzled inquiry.

'You are trailing the hook for Nico, aren't you?' Leo watched her from the shelter of the broad-brimmed hat he wore, his lips curled in a mocking smile.

She flushed scarlet and glared at him, then turned on her heel and vanished into the house.

His smile became a grimace. His fingers swept the strings with an angry flourish. 'That sister of yours is a feline!'

'Vanessa is rather spoilt,' Nicola agreed. 'She's used to a lot of admiration.'

'What does she do for a living?'

'She's a model.'

'Successful?'

She nodded. 'Very.'

He grimaced again. 'I see! And despises anyone

who's not a financial success? She has an ambitious look when she forgets to smile—a woman's face in repose tells one a great deal. Vanessa's features are potentially exquisite. Her thoughts twist them into grotesque mimicry of beauty.'

'Oh, Leo!' Nicola protested. 'Vanessa is nothing like that!'

'I'm an expert on faces,' he said flatly. 'An artist has to be! I spend my time reading them so that I can put them on canvas. I'm sure I'm right about your sister.'

'You may have grasped a faint part of the truth,' she said slowly. 'Vanessa is ambitious, I agree, but the rest is mere caricature.'

He shrugged. 'Now you have a gentle little face. I'd like to paint you, Nicola. Would you let me?'

She grinned at him. 'After what Domenico said about your ulterior motive?'

'Oh, Nico was pulling your leg!'

'Was he? I rather suspect you're the Don Juan he described.'

Leo laughed, his eyes dancing. 'I adore your English sense of humour, *cara*.'

'Don't change the subject,' she smiled, tongue in cheek. 'Is this a genuine invitation, or are you trying to lure me into your spider's web?'

'Bring Paul and I'll paint you as a Madonna with Child,' he offered solemnly. 'Lorenzo will be highly delighted and pay me a fat fee, and I shall be able to feel a delicious sense of virtue in the process.'

'Paul will be a very effective chaperone,' she agreed.

'He's as sharp-eyed as a wagon-load of monkeys.'

Leo pretended to groan. 'Why did I say it? Why?'

Leo's studio was situated at the top of an old watch-tower which stood on the summit of the hill, over-looking both the Villa and the road down into the valley.

'In the sixteenth century a watch-tower was neces-sary. One's enemies were quite capable of mounting a sudden attack. The Farenze were no more popular than the Medici, although of course we never quite climbed to their heights of power. During the Middle Ages the struggle for eminence somehow left us out on a limb—we didn't have the Medici tenacity, although we had their ambition.'

Nicola watched Leo's face curiously. He had an in-tent light in his dark eyes as he talked about his family. 'You're proud of being a Farenze?'

He grimaced. 'Proud? Can one be proud of belong-ing to a race of cut-throats and bandits? Like any other family we used dirty methods to make our money. Money has that quality—have you noticed? It makes your hands dirty.'

'But all the same you do feel the romance of it,' she insisted with an understanding smile.

He laughed, a little self-deprecatingly. 'You see too much, *mia cara*.'

'You all use that phrase,' she said thoughtfully. '*Mia cara* ... it sounds so much better in Italian. "My dear" in English sounds rather patronising.'

'English is a language which tends to sound pompous,' he said lightly.

'Oh no,' she protested. 'The language of Shakespeare and Milton?'

'And of Queen Victoria and Gladstone, too,' he teased, winking at her.

Nicola was forced to laugh. 'Well——' she conceded, with a little gesture of acceptance. Her neck ached already, she wanted to scratch somewhere around her shoulder blade and her head felt so heavy that she was half afraid it would fall off at any moment. Sitting for one's portrait was by no means an enjoyable experience, she decided somewhat ruefully.

Leo paused, eyeing her. 'Tired?'

'Exhausted,' she admitted.

'Like a short break?'

'It would be heavenly!'

He grinned and laid his brush down on the tall stool behind him. 'Right, then. Come and have some coffee.'

Stretching, her muscles almost squeaking after their enforced inactivity, she gave a groan of delight. 'Coffee? What a delightful thought. Shall I make it?'

He shook his head, unscrewing a flask he produced from a covered basket lying among the litter which lay everywhere in the studio.

'I made it before you got here.' He poured her some steaming black coffee into a china mug, added a little milk from a bottle which stood in a corner. Nicola accepted the mug gratefully, inhaling the delicious fragrance as if it were the odour of nectar.

'Can I see what you've done so far?' she asked.

Leo sharply shook his head. 'No! I prefer the sitter to wait until I've finished. Once you've seen the picture you change your attitude. I don't just paint your body, you know—I'm trying to get your essential spirit on to the canvas. I've known a sitter be so incensed by what I'd painted that he put up the shutters for the other sittings, and I could not see anything of what he was thinking or feeling. The only emotion I could get was this great black cloud of rage between us.'

'So you painted that?' Her tongue-in-cheek question made him grin at her, flipping a long index finger against her cheek.

'You can be quite wickedly perceptive in your way, Nicola! Yes, I painted that.'

Her lashes lifted suddenly and she looked at him shrewdly. 'Was that Nico?'

Leo's brows rose into an arc of astonished amusement. 'Yes, it was!' He spoke in English, but with that delightfully grave Italian intonation. 'How did you guess that, I wonder?'

'From his attitude to you. I wonder what it was you saw that made him so angry?'

Leo shrugged. '*Mia cara*, I do not even know myself. When I paint I am not consciously interpreting what I see—I merely paint intuitively. Whatever it was that angered Nico was something I had seen with my eyes but not comprehended with my brain. He saw it, and felt ...' he lifted his hands, grimacing, 'what shall I say? Naked?'

116

Nicola was thoughtful as she returned to the house later. Looking back, she saw Leo at his studio window, at the top of the old tower, wearing a black shirt splashed with many colours, daubed when he wiped his brush against his chest. He raised a hand in mimed greeting. For a second she saw him as a wizard in a fairy story, at the tower window, conjuring up storms. Leo had something of that dangerous quality. Things happened around him. Whether by chance, or the accident of his nature, or because some deep native mischief in him made him enjoy causing trouble, Leo created situations which were potentially stormy.

What had he seen in Domenico's face?

Domenico had objected strongly when Leo first broached the idea of painting Nicola and Paul as a Madonna and Child. His face dark with rage, he said the idea was ludicrous.

'Leo couldn't paint such a subject without being blasphemous,' he told Lorenzo.

The old man was studying Leo soberly. 'You think you can do this, Leo? You think it will be good?'

Leo was serious for once. 'I have a feeling, Lorenzo.' He held out his hands, their long tips steady. 'Here . . . I feel certain it is what I must do.'

Domenico laughed harshly. 'Dramatic nonsense! You should have been an actor, Leo. You missed your vocation.'

'Nico!' Lorenzo looked at him in surprised reproach.

'Nico, Leo has talent. If he will take this seriously, it could be a picture worth hanging on our walls.'

'Of course,' Domenico said stiffly, 'if it pleases you, Lorenzo, there is no more to be said. You must do as you wish. My own opinion is that Leo is up to one of his tricks.'

Nicola decided, at that point, to intervene, in the hope of bringing some sort of peace.

'Whether the picture is good or not, it will be fun,' she said lightly, smiling at Lorenzo. 'Paul and I will enjoy it enormously. I've never had my portrait painted before. It will be a new experience.'

Domenico's lip curled at the edges in a faint sneer. 'Oh, it will be that, no doubt,' he said sardonically.

Later, finding him alone in the courtyard before dinner, she had tentatively broached the subject once more, only to find him still bitterly opposed.

'I can't see that it will do any harm,' she had said in mild bewilderment.

His glance was cool and sharp. 'Your marriage seems to have left you strangely innocent.'

She had flushed. 'What has my marriage to do with this painting?'

'It is not your image only that Leo has designs on,' he had said cuttingly.

'Oh!' She had been silent for a moment. 'Well, of course, I know his reputation. But I am a grown woman, you know. I've been responsible for myself for years—I know how to cope with most techniques. Men have tried all sorts of tactics in the past—from the sad, little-boy-lost approach to the sweep-you-off-your-feet-before-you-have-time-to-realise-what's-happening approach. I've seen them all, at one time or another, and I know all the answering moves.' Her green eyes glowed up at him, wide with laughter. 'Leo will have to be pretty expert to take me in, I promise you.'

'Oh, he will?' Domenico sounded odd, staring down at her with narrowed eyes. Before she had guessed his intention he had seized her wrists, pulling her close to him, so that she overbalanced and fell against him, her hands wriggling in his grip.

'Don't be ridiculous, let me go!' she cried angrily.

He bent his head and sought her mouth, and twist and struggle though she did, he found and held it briefly, his lips hard and hot against hers.

She felt a sweet, drowning happiness. Then she was free, her lids still flickering with startled surprise. Domenico stood back from her, his hands pushed down into his pockets.

'You were saying?'

She glared at him, angry that she had been so aroused by his meaningless kiss. How dared he behave like that?

'Yes,' she said scathingly, 'brute force is the one technique which is hard to counter, but then I don't see Leo as the brute type. Unlike you, he's more likely to use persuasion than force.'

119

She was glad to see dark colour rising into his face. At least she had managed to sting him!

When she reached the Villa, after her walk back from Leo's tower, she found Lorenzo and Paul in the garden together, bouncing a ball. Lorenzo's great age and Paul's youth made them both a little uncertain of their strength and occasionally unsteady on their feet. They were ideally suited as playmates, and Nicola was deeply moved by the sheer quiet happiness she saw in the old man's lined face. He was enjoying a sort of Indian summer in the companionship of his beloved grandson.

She waved to them, and they waved back cheerfully. 'I'm going to change for lunch,' she said. She wore one of Vanessa's dresses for her sittings, since it was just the shade of blue which Leo had wanted her to wear, and had a full, yet simple, cut which was very suitable for the subject.

In the cool, marble hall she found Domenico talking to one of the other servants and Angelina. Domenico dismissed them with a nod, and turned to look at her in a level, measuring way which made her chin rise in defiance immediately.

'How are the sittings going?'

The question sounded innocuous enough, but she knew that it was calculated to provoke her. 'Very well,' she answered in the same cool style.

His glance flicked her from head to foot. 'That dress does not exactly make you look like a virgin mother.'

120

She shrugged. 'It's the right colour. That's all Leo wanted.'

'All?' The tone was sardonic.

She lifted innocent green eyes to his face. 'Yes,' she said softly, then turned to go upstairs.

His hand caught her elbow and she looked round. His face was oddly uncertain, the eyes half hooded by his lids. 'Nicola,' he said huskily.

Her heart seemed to stop, then go on beating much faster, leaving her oddly trembling and pale. 'Yes?' she managed to ask in a faint whisper.

The click of a heel on the marble floor broke the brief spell and his hand dropped from her elbow. Blindly, on impulse, she fled up the stairs without another word. As she turned the bend on to the first landing she caught a glimpse of Bianca, golden and vibrant, staring across the hall. Domenico had vanished.

Nicola changed with fumbling fingers. The bell which summoned the household to lunch was rung violently while she was just doing up her last button.

She gave herself a fleeting glance in the mirror and ran to the door. It opened as she reached it and Violetta, the cook, smiled shyly at her from the corridor. She was a cheerful, plump woman of fifty, with white-tipped dark wings of hair curved across the top of her head and capable, dimpled brown hands.

'*Signora,*' she began breathlessly, 'tomorrow is my brother's feast day, and I wondered if you would permit me to make a cold lunch before I go so that I may take the whole day?'

'Of course,' Nicola agreed warmly. She had taken over some of the household arrangements from Signora Farenze, at her own suggestion, and had for several days been giving the cook her orders. Aunt Francesca had insisted that Nicola was far better able to choose a menu, and order the food, having been trained for the task. Glad to be of help, Nicola had attempted to be tactful with the cook, who, after all, had been cooking at the villa for a long time. Nicola suddenly had an idea which pleased her.

'Cook, it would be a better plan if you did not have to do any work on your brother's feast day—then you could leave here tonight and be at home for the whole day. I will do all the cooking tomorrow.'

Violetta's eyes grew round with astonishment and reproof. 'You, *signora*? That is not suitable.'

'Why not? I'm a cook! I am not an expert on Italian food, but I think I could make an eatable meal for the family just for once.'

Violetta was struggling for expression, her lips trembling. 'You will do my job, *signora*?'

Nicola suddenly realised that Violetta feared to lose her position at the villa. She laughed and patted the other woman's hand in reassurance. 'Oh, I couldn't do your job for more than one day, Violetta!' She spread her hands wide in emphasis. 'Your job is quite safe, don't worry.'

Violetta sighed with relief. 'Then thank you, *signora*. I shall be grateful to go tonight. I see so little of my family, and this will be a great family gathering. You are very kind.'

She turned to go, curtseying. A moment later Nicola, having given a last look around her room to make sure she had not left anything, followed her, in time to hear a peculiar confusion of sounds out of which she managed to fish first a wild cry in Italian, then a thud, followed by a number of bumps and bangs mixed somehow with the sound of a bouncing ball.

She ran to the stairs. Violetta was just landing at the bottom, her skirts flying, her arms waving in desperate search of some hold.

By the time Nicola had reached her, the rest of the household were there, too. Violetta was white with pain. Domenico, gently examining her where she sat on the marble floor, said with a grim look that she had broken her arm.

'Broken her arm? Oh, poor Violetta!' Nicola knelt beside her. 'We must get a doctor at once.'

'Hospital,' Domenico said crisply. 'I'll take her in my car. She'll have to have the arm put in plaster.'

'But the pain . . .' Violetta was groaning piteously.

'Driving might be excruciatingly painful,' Nicola told her. 'I suppose the doctor couldn't come and give her an injection to stop the pain before we drive her to hospital?'

Domenico went to the telephone, speaking calmly, then came back. 'The doctor is out on a case. We have no alternative but to take her into Florence at once.'

123

'Cushions,' Nicky said urgently. 'We need cushions to support the arm.' She flew off to find some.

When she returned with an armful of fat cushions, she found Domenico holding a glass of brandy to Violetta's pallid lips. The servant was drinking it meekly.

'Oh, good idea,' Nicola congratulated him. 'That should be a help.'

She went out to arrange the cushions in Domenico's car. Vanessa, Bianca and Lorenzo stood, helplessly, watching the scene. Vanessa detested any form of illness or pain. She was quite pale herself, merely from watching Violetta's agony.

'Let her rest here for a moment before we try to move her,' said Domenico when Nicola returned to the hall. 'The brandy will need time to work. I gave her a pretty powerful dose.' He spoke in English so that Violetta should not understand him. 'She'll be out like a light if she isn't used to it.'

Indeed, Violetta was looking a little better already, her colour returning slightly and the strained agony of her features much less pronounced.

'How the hell did it happen?' Domenico looked up the stairs. 'What made her fall?'

'It must have been this,' said Bianca, surprisingly, pointing to Paul's red ball, which lay in a corner of the hall. 'I saw it roll away from the stairs as I ran out. She must have fallen over it.' She gave Nicola a sullen look. 'I've told Paul how dangerous it is to leave his ball lying about where people can fall over it, but he does need to be watched to make sure he does these things. If his mother isn't ever with him, how can he learn?'

'I heard the ball bouncing as Violetta fell,' Nicola admitted unhappily. 'I'm so sorry if it was Paul's fault. I'll speak to him about it and get him to see how serious it is.'

Lorenzo's voice struck in harshly. He did not look at Bianca. 'It could not have been Paul who put the ball on the stairs. He and I came in together and I saw Angelina take him upstairs. I myself placed the ball on the table over there.'

'Paul must have come down again to fetch it,' Bianca said in a shrill voice, looking suddenly pale.

Lorenzo turned his head slowly and looked at her, his eyes stony.

'Angelina would never permit the child to go up or come down the stairs without her. It is impossible.'

Bianca drew a ragged breath. 'No, well, it is ... perhaps it was not the ball, then. Violetta may have just slipped ...'

Violetta raised her head weakly. 'It was the ball.' She looked at Lorenzo. 'It was in the shadows ... I could not see it there.'

'There was only Nicola upstairs?' Lorenzo sounded heavy and regretful.

Nicola looked at him in astonishment. 'I didn't leave the ball on the stairs! Why on earth should I?'

Lorenzo inclined his head. 'Indeed, *mia cara*. Why on earth should anyone deliberately leave a ball on the stairs for someone to trip over?'

CHAPTER EIGHT

THEY drove Violetta into Florence as soon as she was sufficiently tranquillised by the brandy. Even so, Nicola had to sit with her in the back of the car, gently soothing her, as she lay back, surrounded by cushions but wincing every time Domenico went over a bump in the road.

The roads down into Florence from the hills were old and not too well attended to—for all Domenico's care it was inevitable that Violetta should suffer a little.

They were all grateful and relieved when she could finally be handed over to a doctor at the hospital. She was not too badly injured, apart from her broken arm, and when she insisted on being sent to her own home from the hospital in time for her brother's feast day, Domenico left instructions at a local taxi office that she should be picked up and driven home whenever the hospital were able to discharge her.

During the drive back to the villa Nicola was silent in her seat. It seemed so far-fetched to imagine that someone had left a ball on the stairs deliberately, in order to cause an accident, but as Lorenzo had said, what alternative was there? The ball could not have

126

bounced up the stairs into the darkest part. Someone had put it there. Who?

She already knew the answer, of course. Bianca. The other girl had betrayed herself in every look, every word.

Why had she done it? Nicola shivered, imagining what might have resulted from such an accident. They had been lucky. Violetta had only broken her arm, but it might have been her neck.

Lorenzo had said no more after his cryptic few remarks about the possibilities. He had turned and stalked back into the dining-room. Vanessa, wide-eyed and curious, had given her sister a long, inquiring look, then followed the old man. What had happened to Bianca? Nicola could not remember. She had been too stunned to notice. Her mind had been too busy trying to take in just what had happened, and all the implications of it.

Domenico drew the car suddenly in to the side of the road. She blinked up at him.

'Why are you stopping?'

'We both need a drink,' he said curtly.

Then she realised that they had parked near an inn. Stiffly, she climbed out of the car and followed him into the shadowy interior. The proprietor came out, wiping his hands on a white apron, and smiled at them. '*Buon giorno!* What can I get you?'

Domenico spoke to him in Italian, smiling. The man nodded and vanished, returning with a bottle and two glasses.

They sat down at a table near the open door. Pine

127

trees cast a deep shadow over the dusty white road. A pigeon somewhere whirred softly. They were the only customers. The siesta heat kept everyone indoors. The proprietor, with a smile, sank down into a chair and dozed lightly.

Domenico drank the red wine with a stern expression on his face. Sipping hers slowly, Nicola wondered if he was angry with her, and why. Was it possible that he did believe she had left the ball on the stairs?

'We shall have to find someone else to cook,' he said abruptly. 'I'll get Angelina to choose someone.'

'Why not me?' she asked.

He looked at her in astonishment. 'You?'

She smiled. 'I am a cook, remember? I would enjoy doing the cooking for a while. I can brush up my Italian recipes.'

'It's ridiculous,' he said curtly. 'Out of the question.'

Her spine stiffened. 'Why?'

'You're a member of the family, not a servant,' he snapped.

'I am a cook; professionally,' she snapped back. 'You don't think Lorenzo would object, do you? He didn't mind Leo painting my portrait. Why should he mind *me* cooking his dinner?'

'That was different.'

'I don't see how.'

'Then you must be blind,' he said coldly.

'Explain it to me, then. Enlighten me.' She used a tone every bit as sarcastic as his own.

'Lorenzo's pride would be hurt—it's as simple as

that. You are the mother of his grandson. If people got to hear that you'd worked in his kitchen as a cook, he would be ashamed.'

'But that's ridiculous!'

He shrugged. 'Possibly!'

'It's downright archaic,' she said angrily .

He gave her a cool look. 'That is your opinion. You are not a proud old man who is desperately clinging on to the last shreds of family glory.'

'We'll see,' she said in a tone of calm determination. 'I'll speak to Lorenzo myself. I think I can make him see sense.'

Domenico laughed. 'You are almost as myopic as Lorenzo is, aren't you?'

Nicola was baffled. 'What? I don't understand you.'

'No,' he murmured under his breath. 'You're right —you don't.'

Lorenzo was at first astounded, then horrified, then, as she coaxed and pleaded, mildly hurt.

'But, *mia cara*, it is not right that you should work as a servant in my house when you are its rightful mistress.'

Cunningly, she smiled down at him. 'If I am rightful mistress then I may do as I choose, Lorenzo. It would make me happy to cook for you and Paul. I like cooking.' She gestured. 'It's hard to explain, but it satisfies something deep inside me.'

The leonine old head nodded sagely. 'You are a woman. It is your nature to like to cherish and feed your family. Ah, *cara*, I understand now.' With equal cunning, he peered up at her. 'But when will you call me Pappa, daughter?'

'When I am cooking for you in my own kitchen, Pappa,' she said, laughing at him.

He threw back his head and roared with delight. 'You are all female—how I regret the years I lost by my blind folly in rejecting you at first!'

Her dark hair shone as she bent her head to kiss his withered cheek. 'Never regret, Pappa. Let us just enjoy what we have now.'

He looked at her with deep pleasure, admiring the gentle curve of her mouth and cheek, the bloom of her tanned skin, the whiteness of her neck, and her smiling green eyes.

'*Mia cara*, you must marry again. It is wicked to waste such loveliness on a child and an old man. You were formed for love.'

Nicola blushed and laughed. 'Time enough for that! I'm not past my first youth yet, I hope.'

'You will not make the mistake of loving Leo?' He looked at her anxiously. 'Leo is gay and charming, but he is not serious enough for you, *mia cara*.'

'Leo is my friend,' she said gently. 'No more than that, I promise you. I like him, that's all.'

Lorenzo sighed deeply. 'Good, that is reassuring. I have worried about it. Domenico spoke to me, warning me about allowing Leo to see so much of you . . .'

'Oh, he did, did he?' Her tone was indignant. The green eyes spat fire.

Lorenzo looked at her casually, then with narrowed eyes. His mouth curved. 'So ... He relaxed with a smile. 'So ...'

His tone alerted her, and she stared at him, suddenly wary. What did he mean by that expression? she wondered. But her probing glance could not read his thoughts. The wrinkled features smiled amiably, but hid their secrets.

There was general surprise and consternation when the rest of the household discovered that Lorenzo had agreed that Nicola might take over the cooking until Violetta was better.

Vanessa was outspoken in her disgust. 'Are you mad, sweetie? I thought the idea was to make the old man forget that you were ever a cook. He'll despise you for offering to work in the kitchen—he'll think it's where you really belong. And others will think so, too—and say it out loud.'

Nicola laughed. 'Bianca?'

'Who else?' Vanessa's voice was thin with anger. 'She makes me so mad I could scream! She looks straight through me half the time, as if I was invisible, and when she does notice me it's just to be really unpleasant. Snobbish, spiteful little cat! I'd hate to give her an excuse for sneering at us.'

'Why take any notice of her?' Nicola asked quietly. 'She's very young, and rather silly. I think she feels rather uncertain of herself underneath all that arrogance.'

'You have to be kidding!' Vanessa laughed in a hard way.

Nicola shook her head. 'I'm serious, Van.'

'Don't call me that! You know I hate it.'

'I'm sorry. I'll try to remember, but childhood habits die hard, and I always did call you Van when we were little, didn't I? Don't you remember?'

'Of course I remember,' her sister snapped. 'I've always tried to stop you using that ridiculous childhood nickname, but you were as stubborn then as you are now.'

'I don't mean to be stubborn,' Nicola sighed. 'It is just that I do love cooking, and I feel useless when I'm not doing something.'

'You've got time to spare for Paul now,' Vanessa pointed out. 'That isn't being useless, is it?'

'Paul has Angelina waiting on him hand and foot. I see more of him than I used to do, but Angelina does all the work. I just play with him.'

'I give up,' groaned Vanessa. 'You sound as though work was sacred!'

Nicola laughed. 'In a way that is what I think,' she admitted with amusement. 'We're like machines. If we aren't in regular use we rust and decay.'

'I'm not getting rusty,' said Vanessa, looking down at her own long brown legs with satisfaction. 'I'm having the time of my life here. I sunbathe, read magazines, relax—it's the best holiday I've ever had. The only time you ever sit down for more than two minutes is when you're sitting to Leo.' She shot Nicola a cool, blue-eyed look. 'He isn't going to be pleased if you're in the kitchen all day. How can he paint you then?'

'He'll have to paint you instead,' Nicola said lightly. 'After all, ever since we got here we've heard how very paintable you are, Vanessa.'

Vanessa flushed angrily and gave her a fierce glare. 'Sit for Leo? I'd rather do the cooking!'

Leo's mocking voice came from the door. 'My God, a fate worse than death!'

Vanessa spun, suddenly pink to her very hair. Her blue eyes stabbed at him across the room. 'Eavesdroppers hear no good of themselves—didn't you know?'

'Another cliché, *mia cara*. What a very limited little mind you have!'

Nicola was puzzled by the cruelty in his voice. Did Leo really detest her sister that much? She looked at Vanessa unhappily. Was it her imagination, or had her sister winced at Leo's words?

Vanessa gave a bright, hard little smile. 'Not too limited to see your little game, Michelangelo! Nicola will be very rich when Lorenzo dies, won't she?'

Leo's eyes narrowed to dark, mocking slits. 'I think you have misunderstood the situation, my dear.' His English was formal and oddly grave. 'Everything is for Paul. Nicola will merely be a trustee. Dear Domenico, also, I believe.'

'But any man who married her would hold a whip over Domenico's head,' Vanessa purred.

Leo pretended surprise. 'Why, so he would!'

133

'And you would love to do that, wouldn't you?' Vanessa added with a long, smiling glance.

He bowed sardonically. 'How well you read my mind! Almost one would think we thought alike.'

There was a silence, then she turned on her heel and left the room, banging the door behind her.

'Must you tease her like that, Leo?' Nicola was disturbed by the scene she had just witnessed. 'Vanessa doesn't have much of a sense of humour, I'm afraid. She may seem very lighthearted, but she takes life seriously.'

'Seriously?' Leo laughed. 'Please, *mia cara*, do not make me laugh so much. It hurts.'

'I don't think you understand Vanessa. She wants a great deal from life.'

'Money? Clothes? Parties? I had noticed.' His voice was coolly sardonic, and there was a bitter twist to his lips. 'She is not hard to understand, *cara*.'

'Have you ever asked yourself why she wants those things so badly?' Nicola was sober. 'Because when she was young she was rather hurt by the first man she ever loved. He was callous and selfish. After that Vanessa was determined to succeed, to be secure. She's never talked to me about it, but I watched the change in her. She was always gay and fond of fun, but she hardened after she'd broken with this man. Now she thinks money solves everything.'

Leo watched her face thoughtfully, frowning. 'You have much fondness for her?'

'She's my sister. She puzzles me at times, but I sup-

134

pose I have a basic feeling of concern for her.'

He grinned. 'In other words, you are fond of her, but she often slaps you away when you try to show it?'

She sighed. 'I'm afraid that's more or less the case, yes. Vanessa isn't very demonstrative.'

Leo nodded. After a moment he asked, 'What is all this about you taking over in the kitchen? You aren't serious?'

'I certainly am!'

'But what about my portrait of you? How can I finish it if you are forever cooking?'

'I shall fit an hour or so into the morning routine,' she said easily. 'I shall need a day or two to get used to the kitchen. but after that I've no doubt I shall find time to spare for you.'

He grimaced. 'You make me sound like the dentist! I have worked hard on this portrait. It is important to me.'

'More important than food?'

He grinned. 'You forget, I cook my own meals. I've a modern kitchen in the tower.'

'What do you cook?' She was curious. 'I can't imagine you as a culinary genius.'

'I am superb,' he said modestly. 'I can do an excellent spaghetti. My salads are crisp and delicious. I make a superb tomato and beef sauce.'

She laughed. 'I'm very impressed. What else?'

'Else? What more is necessary?' He looked offended. 'Salad and spaghetti—the basic stuffs of life. I live like a king.'

135

'Mmmm ...' She eyed him reprovingly. 'I had noticed! Tell me, Leo, do you sell your paintings?'

His dark eyes danced. 'Suspicious female! Yes, I do, quite frequently.'

'Do they sell well?'

'Are you investigating my income for the revenue people, or is this a personal interest?'

She flushed. 'I'm sorry, it was rude of me. I was just interested.'

'Why?' He was suddenly serious.

'Why?' She shrugged. 'Just vulgar curiosity, I suppose, and a certain concern for you. It would be painful to paint pictures one couldn't sell. I'm glad you sell them.'

He watched her, head on one side. 'Nicola,' he murmured uneasily, 'you aren't getting ... well, how can I put it? Interested in me?'

She laughed at his wary expression. 'Poor Leo, did you suddenly feel the breath of pursuit on your neck? No, I'm not in full chase. You can relax. My concern was as sisterly as my feeling towards Vanessa.'

He gave her an amused grin. 'Well, I'm not certain that that is a complimentary remark, but I think I'll take it as being meant for one. And seriously, Nicola—I'm glad you and I can be just good friends. I would hate to hurt you, but I have never seen you in any more intimate light.'

'Nor I you, Leo,' she said cheerfully. 'So we can both forget it, can't we?'

He bent his head and kissed her lightly on the mouth.

As he raised his head again he smiled down at her. 'Sweet, sweet Nicky, I am so glad you came to the Villa.'

As they moved apart Nicola caught sight of Bianca in the courtyard watching them with an intent, unreadable expression. The other girl flushed as Nicola's eyes met hers, then, turning on her heel, she hurried away.

That evening they had a simple dinner of soup and a mixed fish salad; anchovy, prawn, shrimps, with cold rice moulded into a ring filled with a smooth white sauce flavoured with mushroom and onions.

The next morning Nicola started work in earnest, poring over cookery books for an hour before she decided on the various meals she would make in the next few days. She always liked to plan ahead so that she could use any left-overs for a meal on the following day. Minestrone was a particularly useful way of using meat or vegetables left from the previous day.

By the third morning she felt that she could afford to leave the kitchen for an hour or two in the morning so as to sit for Leo. Her first two days as cook had been highly successful. She had served veal escalopes and canelloni, veal in a white sauce wrapped in pancakes and a filling bowl of perfectly cooked spaghetti with a sauce made from tomatoes, mushrooms, beef and herbs. Each meal had gone well. She felt that she had proved herself and could now relax.

In a way, she thought, as she walked across the green lawns to the old tower, the spaghetti had been the most demanding dish to cook. The sheer simplicity of it made it essential that it be exactly right. No Italian would miss a mistake in the cooking of spaghetti. She might disguise a slip in her veal or canelloni—but not in spaghetti.

It pleased her that Lorenzo had said, 'And now shall we have some English cooking, *mia cara*? Some soggy pudding and underdone beef?' His mellow laughter had delighted her, despite the insult to her national dish.

'If you would like to try some English dishes,' she had said, tongue in cheek, 'you certainly shall! I shall be delighted to cook them for you, Pappa!'

The whole table had reacted to that deliberate use of the name. Bianca had stiffened and cast her a dark-eyed look. Domenico's head had come up, the grey eyes narrowed. Leo, invited especially for that meal, had grinned and winked, while Vanessa had given her a smile of approval. Even Signora Farenze, frail as a tiny bird in her chair, had seemed surprised.

Lorenzo had been enchanted, not least by the way everyone else reacted. He was not yet past the pleasure of making people stare in astonishment or reproof; and it amused him to see that the growing affection between himself and Nicola had a profound effect upon the rest of the family.

He said to her, later, when they were alone, 'I like to make them jump! It proves to me, as well as to them, that I can still make my mark on life. When I was a young man I had a fine time with the girls. Then I discovered the joys of business, the power politics of

138

the financial world. I am past them now, money and girls both. I sometimes wake up in the night and pinch myself just to make sure I am not dead. But you and Paul have given me a new lease of life, *mia cara*. I can feel the sap in my veins again.'

'Don't overdo it,' she said with a scolding note. 'You were running about with Paul for too long yesterday.'

'Running?' He laughed loud and long at that. 'Did I run, *cara*? You astonish me!'

'Promise me not to tire yourself,' she pleaded. 'I know you're enjoying yourself, but slow down a little. You'll enjoy life even longer if you do.'

'Domenico has spoken to you! He is more of an old woman than his mother!' Lorenzo was sulky, like a little boy whose new toy was being snatched away.

'We love you,' she said gently. 'That's all!'

The leonine head lifted proudly. 'So? Is that true, *cara*?' And at her smiling nod, he shrugged. 'Then how can I have the coldness to resist? I will be more careful, for your sake, Nicola, if not for my own!'

Leo saw her approaching across the grass and waved to her from his tower window, leaning down to smile and call a greeting.

'How nice, Nicola,' he said as she came into the studio, a little breathless from the stairs. 'I am so glad you could come this morning.'

She flopped into the chair he had placed for her on the raised dais. In the finished portrait she was to hold Paul on her lap, but for the moment they were using a doll as a model since Paul was not easy to keep still for any long period, and was merely a noisy distraction to Leo.

Leo arranged the pose once more, coolly adjusting her arms and the tilt of her head to suit himself. 'Lean back a little ... yes ...' He stood back and studied her dispassionately, looking more like a surgeon than an artist.

The thought made her grin, and he looked quizzically at her. She told him her thought in a light tone.

'You looked as if you were deciding which arm to cut off rather than how best to pose me!'

'Surgeons and artists have a similar education in one way,' Leo said gravely. 'They need a good idea of anatomy, and they must take into account the patient's state of mind as well as his body.'

'And they often make enemies after the event,' she added in a half-serious voice.

Leo nodded, smiling. 'That is certainly true of artists —I'm not sure about surgeons, but I imagine people often resent them. We both of us see too much of the truth about people. The human mind detests being seen so clearly.'

Nicola was silent, staring at the blue sky which was all that she could see from the window. They were way above the level of the trees in this room. To see the ground one had to stand at the window and look down, and she suddenly wondered if that was not dangerous —looking down on the rest of the world created a false sense of superiority in people. Perhaps that explained the arrogance of the medieval men who had built this place!

A voice broke in upon the absorbed silence in which Leo liked to work. He groaned and laid down his brush.

'Bianca!'

Nicola looked round with an embarrassed feeling of uneasiness. She always felt that Bianca disliked her, and being in her presence was not a pleasant experience. The other girl seemed to stare with such hostility! Nicola knew perfectly well that she had no need to feel guilty. She and Paolo had loved each other. Yet Bianca's cold stare always made her feel that she had in some way hurt her by marrying Paolo. Bianca was a girl whose loyalties were simple and tenacious. She loved Barbara, the girl who should have married Paolo, and she would not forgive Nicola for having hurt the other girl, even unknowingly.

Bianca came into the room and stopped dead at the sight of Nicola.

There was a cold silence, then Leo grimaced. 'Well, little sister? What do you want?'

Turning from her antagonistic contemplation of Nicola, the other girl tossed her head. 'To speak with you—alone!'

Leo threw her an angry look. 'Very well, you ill-mannered little shrew! Nicola, *cara*, you will excuse me? And excuse, too, my bad little sister who should be beaten for her insolence if my father were not so many miles away in South America?'

141

Bianca snapped, 'Do not dare to apologise for me, Leo! And to her ...'

'I would apologise to the devil if you treated him as you treat Nicola,' he said sternly. 'You are a fool, Bianca, and an ill-bred one, too.'

Bianca flounced from the room without answering, and with a sigh Leo followed her, telling Nicola to seize the chance of relaxing for a few moments.

She got up, stretched herself and began to wander around the room, inspecting the various half-finished or finished paintings. They were either very modernistic or in a purely representational style—either wild explosions of colour and shape, or portraits of perfectly recognisable people. Obviously Domenico had been a trifle harsh when he dismissed Leo's portraits as un-representational. Or had Leo deliberately teased him into this belief? She knew Leo well enough by now to know that he was capable of such behaviour. Leo rather resented Domenico's special status at the villa. They were both cousins, equally closely related to Lorenzo, and Leo felt that Domenico had an unfair advantage in that he had gone into the wine business while Leo had become an artist. This had made Domenico decidedly the favourite of Lorenzo, and a power at court.

On a desk near the window stood a box of sharp pencils and a loosely tied portfolio. Nicola idly picked at the knot and it fell apart, the papers fluttering out. She managed to shuffle them back into their pile, and then her busy fingers were stilled as she realised, with astonished wonder, that she was gazing at some superb pencil drawings of Vanessa.

Leo had used the finest pencils, the most delicate lines, never explicit, always implying tentatively. Vanessa's hair seemed to flow, like coiled snakes or eddying water, around a face of exquisite purity.

Only a closer inspection revealed other facets of the drawings. The eyes were perfectly shaped—yet held fathoms of meaning within their depths. Cold knowledge, snake-like, secret. The mouth was parted on a gentle sigh, yet hinted at cruelty and greed in the sweet, fine curves.

Leo had deliberately invested the pictures with a burning intensity. Innocence and purity formed the shell within which he sketched selfishness and corruption. Vanessa looked like a fallen angel.

Transfixed, enraged and astonished, Nicola stared at one after another of the drawings. When had he drawn them? Why had he drawn them? Only a bitter hostility could explain away the way in which he had invested Vanessa with such terrible qualities.

A step on the stairs made her turn, a drawing in her hand. Leo stopped dead in the doorway, staring.

'How could you?' She was too angry to speak clearly, her voice stammered out words. 'So unkind ... untrue ... if she ever saw them she would be so hurt!'

Leo walked across the room in silence. He took the portfolio from her, deftly pushed the drawings into place and tied the knot tightly.

'No one need ever have seen them if you had not pried, like Pandora,' he said curtly.

She acknowledged the justice of that. 'I'm sorry if I overstepped the line. I didn't know you would mind. You've let me see other drawings, other paintings.'

'I would not have left these out if I had known you were coming this morning,' he said, putting the portfolio into a wall cupboard and carefully locking the door.

'But, Leo, why have you done them?' Bewilderment made her ask him.

'Can we change the subject?' His voice was sharp. 'Leave me some private corners of my life!'

Nicola flushed at the snub and returned to the dais, but the spell of their earlier session was broken. Leo painted for a while, but he seemed uncertain, and at last he flung down his brush with a black look.

'Oh, clear off!' He spoke in terse English. 'The day is ruined. I can't paint today.'

CHAPTER NINE

NICOLA was soaking leaves of lasagne verde when Vanessa sauntered into the kitchen, her slender body sheathed in elegant black pants and a fragile white chiffon blouse which looked as if it had been spun by spiders.

'You look gorgeous,' Nicola said appreciatively.

Vanessa shrugged, for once indifferent to a compliment. 'Nicky, I think I'll go home tomorrow.'

Nicola dropped two leaves of the pasta together and muttered irritably as she tried to separate them before they became irretrievably welded. When she had achieved this, she looked round at her sister incredulously. 'Are you serious?'

Vanessa flushed and avoided her gaze. 'Quite serious.'

'But why? Is something wrong? Someone upset you?' Then, quickly, 'Bianca?'

Vanessa laughed. 'Bianca? You must be kidding! She couldn't affect me by one jot or tittle.'

'Then why? I thought you were enjoying yourself.'

Her sister fiddled vaguely with a bowl of eggs, fol-

145

lowing their shape with one finger. 'I suppose I'm homesick.'

Unconvinced, Nicola said softly, 'What is it, Van? I can see you're really unhappy. What's wrong?'

'I ... I don't know.' Vanessa twisted a strand of curly golden hair and began to bite it, like a schoolgirl. Nicola could remember when her sister used to do this during their childhood, and the sight made her feel protective and alarmed. Surely something must have gone seriously wrong for Vanessa to lose her poise.

Had Vanessa, by some ghastly chance, seen Leo's drawings of her?

When had Leo done those drawings, anyway? By stealth? Or from memory? She had never seen him openly drawing Vanessa. The two of them had been sharply antagonistic ever since the first day.

'If you told me I might be able to help,' she said gently. Her sister looked at her, almost hopelessly, her blue eyes round and misty. If Leo had ever seen her looking like that, Nicky thought, he would not have drawn those savage portraits of her. We never really know very much about each other. Even close friends can be shocked and surprised to discover some new, unsuspected facet. She knew that Vanessa had never understood anything about her own marriage. Into these areas of one's life one forbids entry even to a sister, and each person sees a different angle of the whole personality.

Vanessa groaned faintly. 'Oh, Nicky! I think ... I think I'm in love.' She said it in tones of horror and revulsion, as if she predicted her own death. For a second Nicky was merely amused. She laughed aloud at the comic expression on her sister's face as she said the words of doom. Then, seeing that Vanessa was hurt by her laughter, she sobered quickly.

Vanessa had turned away in offence. Nicola caught her arm.

'I'm sorry, I shouldn't have laughed. But you looked so funny as you said it!'

'It may be funny to you, but I'm not laughing.' Vanessa sounded stiff in her indignation.

'I can see that,' Nicola agreed gently. 'It's Domenico, of course?'

Vanessa's blue eyes opened wide. 'Domenico? No!' She looked startled.

'No? But . . .' Nicola's voice trailed away as Vanessa looked at her dumbly. 'Oh, no!' she whispered. A spear of understanding shot through her and she winced. 'Not . . . Leo?'

Vanessa silently nodded, biting her lip.

'Leo!' Nicola understood everything now. Of course, Vanessa must be wrenched with pain, knowing that Leo detested her and that her feelings for him were totally unrequited. Vanessa's only other brush with love had been so disastrous, so painful, that fate might have been kinder this time. How tragically ironic that Vanessa, the cool and self-reliant, should fall in love with a man like Leo who despised her.

'I see now why you want to go away,' Nicola nodded.

'I'll speak to Lorenzo. What shall we say? That you have to get back to work?'

'Why not? Any excuse will do. Lorenzo will be in-different—He only wants you and Paul. He won't even notice I've gone—no one will. Least of all L ...' Vanessa broke off, grimacing, tears not far away.

'How long have you ...' Nicola began, then stopped, realising that this was a question she should not ask. Even sisters have no right to pry into the secrets of love.

'The first time I saw him,' Vanessa said grimly. 'He made me so angry, but at the same time he made every-one else look pale and dull. I tried to fall for Domenico. He's quite dishy himself, and he'll be a fantastic husband—but I just couldn't see him. Leo seemed to dominate everything I looked at. It got so bad that I couldn't even sleep. I know he detests me—he shows it plainly enough—but it makes no difference. I feel sick every time I set eyes on him.'

Nicola put her arms around her, forgetting the lasagne verde. Food was of no importance. If the lunch was ruined she would make a salad. One could always ring the changes with a mixture of strange ingredients.

She stroked the blonde curls and Vanessa, for once indifferent to the ruin of her careful make-up, put her head on her sister's shoulder and wept until her mascara had run into little spiky lines down her wet cheeks.

'Must she go at once?' Lorenzo was surprised. 'But I had planned a little surprise for you both—a party!'

He beamed at Nicola, his wrinkles seeming to double as his smile grew.

She was as surprised as he could have wished. 'A party?'

'And you shall not do the cooking, *mia cara*. You have cooked for us so beautifully, but now we shall demand that you permit someone else to do it until Violetta returns. Violetta has a cousin—Anna. She is a widow, a very good cook and cheerful, and she wants to come to us.' He shook his brown index finger at her. 'She needs the money, *cara*. You do not!'

In the face of such an argument, Nicola had no reply. She smiled apologetically. 'That had never occurred to me. I'm sorry. Yes, of course Anna must come.'

Lorenzo was delighted. 'You have impressed us with your skill, *mia cara*. Such sauces!' He bunched his fingers, kissed them with an air. 'And even your soup was always a new experience ... the rich bisque you served yesterday—I was greedy and I suffered for it in the night. I am of an age when greed can be cruel.'

'When will Anna come?' she asked after a few moments.

'She came to see me this morning, to beg for the chance to show what she can do—she knew, of course, that you were cooking, and she said that she would work with you, but I told her that you had only been doing the work until we had decided who to employ in Violetta's place.'

'Cunning Pappa!' said Nicola with amusement.

'She would resent you otherwise,' he said with a

wink. 'I disarmed her hidden resentment, I hope.' He shot her a long look. 'Do you find others who feel like this? Bianca, for instance? Does she behave better now? I spoke to her after the incident of the ball on the stairs. She could have killed someone. I was very stern with her, and I hope I have made her repentant.'

Bianca's hatred might have been pushed underground, thought Nicola, but it was not completely invisible. It showed through at odd moments. Her eyes were always revealing.

'She was very fond of her friend Barbara?' she asked Lorenzo with some curiosity.

'Bianca? Oh, do not believe all she tells you, dear child. It is true that Bianca was fond of Barbara, but there is more to it than that. Bianca was half in love with Paolo herself, I think. She was at an impressionable age. These young girls can feel so deeply! She felt, when he wrote of his marriage to you, that he had slapped her face! Consider, *mia cara*! If Paolo were to disobey me and marry a poor girl, one who worked as a cook—why had he not looked at Bianca, whom he knew very well adored him?' Lorenzo shook his leonine head in pity. 'Poor Bianca! She burned with hatred and with love—and that is why she acts as she does.'

'I did suspect it,' Nicola said slowly. 'Barbara married someone else?'

'Not yet, but she is to do so quite soon, I believe.'

'I heard a rumour that Bianca was to marry Domenico,' she said casually, and waited with painfully held breath for his reply.

150

Lorenzo shrugged. 'Bianca has transferred her emotions to Domenico, it is true. I have thought that they might make a match, but I have ceased to interfere in the affairs of others since you came, *cara*. I made so terrible a mistake over you. Who am I to say who shall marry whom? It would be mere folly.'

'And ... Domenico?' Her voice was husky. Lorenzo glanced at her from beneath lowered lids and smiled, a little cunningly.

'You must ask him yourself, *cara*. Ask him if he is in love.'

Lorenzo had drawn up a list of the guests who were to come to the party he was giving in honour of Nicola herself. He gave it to her, later, and asked her to order some printed invitations from a stationer in Florence who would print the actual names while she waited.

Domenico offered to drive her into the city when he went himself after lunch. His working hours were flexible since he had his office actually in the Villa itself. The clerical staff of the business pursued their duties in an office in Florence, and Domenico commuted between the Villa and Florence. Lorenzo still descended on the firm from time to time, and several other male members of the family worked for the firm, too, but Nicola had not yet met them.

She was to do so when they came to the party, for a large number of the names on the list, she saw, were members of the Farenze family.

It was, she discovered from Domenico on their drive

down into Florence, a widespread family, not all of them people with money. The family instinct is such, in Italy, that there was close contact between them, of whatever social class.

'After all, blood is ...'

'Thicker than water,' she finished for him, with a nod.

He shot her a look. 'We are proud of our past, but we are also proud of our future. We may no longer command the same influence, but Lorenzo still feels a deep affection for everyone of his blood. The children, particularly. He adores children.'

'So I've noticed,' she smiled.

'Paul is special,' he agreed. 'Paul is his own grandson. Lorenzo loves all children, but those of his family mean more.'

'I shall feel as if I'm on display,' Nicola said ruefully. 'They will all come, I suppose?'

'All of them,' he agreed wryly. 'They will flock from the far corners of the earth to see what manner of creature has produced the next Lion of Farenze. Their eyes will strip you to your very bones.'

'Farenze eyes have that capacity,' she nodded drily. 'I've noticed that, too.'

His grey eyes slid sideways to survey her. 'Is that aimed at me?'

'Or Leo,' she added.

'Leo ... Ah, yes, Leo. How is his portrait proceeding? Have you seen it?' His expression had taken on a new cast, a cold sarcasm.

'He will not allow that.'

'How surprising!' The dry tone irritated her.

'But from the other portraits I've seen I have no doubt it will be remarkable. Leo has considerable talent, I think.'

He flipped a quizzical eyebrow. 'You sound defiant. I wonder why?'

'I know you don't agree,' she said crossly.

'You know nothing about me.' The voice hardened, grew strangely alien and offhand.

Nicola was silent for a moment, wondering why he was angry.

Domenico drove on, staring ahead. After a while he asked suddenly, 'Are you in love with Leo?'

She was shaken and looked at him in alarm, her pulses hammering, her skin white with shock. The green eyes widened and filled with unconscious pain.

It was only then, faced with that question, that her brain knew what her heart had known for so long. She was not in love with Leo. No. She was in love with Domenico himself, a love which now, being acknowledged at last, flooded her whole being with a stinging emotion, compounded of joy and hurt.

She had left his question unanswered too long, and Domenico's face tightened. 'I see,' he said coldly. 'I suspected as much.'

'No,' she stammered, hot and trembling, desperate to convince him that he was mistaken. 'No, of course I'm not in love with Leo. I can't think why you should get that impression.'

153

'You need not pretend with me,' he said coolly. 'I know you too well now, Nicola. You went first white, then red, and such violence can only indicate deep emotions. I'm sorry for you. Leo is not the man for you—he'll make you miserable. I warned you at the start, but you wouldn't listen and I knew then that it was useless. You're obstinate and wilful.' His voice dropped the words like icy pebbles into the stream of her mind, and Nicola listened, wincing. How he disliked and despised her!

What was the point of arguing with him? He would believe what he wanted to believe, and it was better for him to believe she loved Leo than to suspect she loved himself.

They were approaching the city now. The cars tore round them, hooting, their drivers leaning out to shout and swear at each other, horns blaring permanently. Italian drivers have a sort of death wish; they drive in perpetual competition, cutting each other out, scraping wheels and bumpers. It is less like a drive along a road than a chariot race updated, with all the violence kept intact.

Only yesterday Lorenzo had shown her a medieval map of Florence hanging on the wall of his library. The blue sky arched overhead, the white bridges, the little huddle of houses fenced in by the old city wall. Ahead of her she saw the modern city, in some ways still faintly reminiscent. The wall still ran here and there, but the city had sprawled out from the walls into the green countryside. There were the landmarks she had come to know and recognise with warmth—the Campanile, the Duomo, the church spires. She felt strangely familiar in this place, as if she had always known it. It was smaller than London, more compact and with a definite centre which all felt with the heart. The Uffizi; the Loggia dei Lanzi, and those beautiful statues which seemed less like the product of man's hands than the genius of nature herself; here one felt the heart of the city beating.

Domenico parked the car and offered to show Nicola the office of the printer, but she refused, politely, wishing to be alone. She wanted to explore further the new world which had opened—to know the limits of her love. What of that old love, her brief marriage with Paolo? How did her love for Domenico measure up to that?

She walked without haste through the narrow, medieval streets, past open doors in which sat old men, women sewing, children playing with gaudy plastic toys. Above her were crumbling walls, windowsills gay with geraniums in boxes and pots, cats perched on high, giddy roofs. The pavements were cracked and sloping. A stall sold early fruit. The vendor shouted in pidgin English as she passed, spotting her nationality in a way which amused her.

It pleased her to find her way, without help, through the maze of little streets. She felt that was really getting to know the city.

The printer was delighted to accept the order, and talked to her as he complied with it, shouting above the rattle and clump of his machinery.

When she left his shop, the invitations safely in her bag, she walked around aimlessly for a while, enjoying the sunshine and the busy life of the city. It was fun to go into a shop and buy some biscuits, speaking Italian so well that the shopkeeper could not quite be certain that she was a foreigner. She beamed at him as she left, enjoying his doubt. She bought chocolate for Paul, a pair of fine leather slippers for Lorenzo at a street stall, for Italian leather goods are both cheap and superb.

When she had realised that it was growing more difficult to get about through the increasing crowds, she made her way back to Domenico's office. He had said he would be there at five o'clock. She found that she was late. He was pacing up and down beside his car looking both annoyed and worried.

He turned on her angrily as she joined him. 'Where the devil have you been? I have been out of my mind. Alone, in a strange city—anything could have happened to you! Why didn't you telephone when you knew you would be late? And what in hell's name have you been doing to be so late?'

Nicola waited until he ran out of breath before replying to this tirade.

'I'm sorry, but I was just exploring. I wanted to see as much of the old city as I could.'

He glared at her, teeth tightly clamped together,

then after a moment he jerked open the door of his car. 'Get in!'

Nicola obeyed meekly. He shot away from the car park as if he were in a race to the moon. She peeped sideways and found him staring at the road ahead, his jaw clenched. There was more to his anger than her late arrival, she decided. Had something happened?

'I should have rung you,' she offered gently. 'I really am sorry, Domenico.'

He glanced at her. 'Oh, forget it,' he said brusquely, the grey eyes cool.

But after a moment or two he began to talk, quite cheerfully, about the old part of Florence, lamenting various changes, and predicting further decay unless some money was spent by the Florentines.

'Italy is going through a bad patch at present. We are falling behind in the industrial race because of inflation and soaring costs ...'

'I know the story,' she groaned. 'You forget, Britain has had the same problems. I sympathise. Inflation is poison.'

They talked about national problems for a while, until the city was left far behind, and the car began the steep climb into the green Tuscan hills.

'Do you now intend to stay in Italy?' He asked the question abruptly.

She hesitated. 'I didn't mean to when I first came, but now that I've got to know Lorenzo I feel somewhat different about the whole thing.'

He nodded. 'Now you know Lorenzo ...' The tone

was dry. 'It has nothing to do with Leo, of course.'

She was surprised that he had brought Leo up again, but she took the chance to deny his belief that she loved Leo.

He listened to her stammered denials impassively. 'You are a little too vehement,' he only said, when she had finished.

'If I want to stay now, it's for Lorenzo and Paul,' she said. 'Lorenzo loves Paul. I was afraid that he would try to treat Paul the way he treated his father, but that hasn't happened.'

'He is very old now, and too aware of the short time he has left,' Domenico agreed. 'He wants only to enjoy Paul's company.'

'That's what I think,' she agreed gently. 'It's wonderful to see them both together. I'm glad I brought Paul, now. He would have missed so much. He has no father to remember, but at least now he will have his grandfather. It will enrich his life.'

He sighed deeply. 'You are wiser than you were, Nicola.'

'Yes,' she said, 'I think I am.'

'And Paolo? Has being here, at the Villa, brought to life his memory for you? Or has Leo pushed him out of your heart at last?'

'At first I thought a great deal about Paolo—naturally,' she agreed. 'But lately I think he has become even more of a memory to me. At last I have laid to rest the ghost of an old bitterness. My resentment towards the

Farenze family had kept grief alive, but that's over now.'

Domenico was silent for a while. 'I can understand that,' he said slowly. 'It is wise of you to put your grief behind you. I am sure you know enough about men to know that any man who married you would feel some jealousy towards your dead husband. After all, you loved him enough to marry him. That would lie between you and anyone else.'

Nicola shivered. 'Only if he felt I didn't love him even more, surely.'

His voice was harsh. 'But could you? How could he believe you loved him more, and how could he bear it if he suspected you loved him less than a dead man?'

'I loved Paolo as a girl loves,' she said passionately.

'And how is that? Tell me?' His voice was cold, merciless, probing her thoughts regardless of how much pain he caused. For a second she almost hated him.

'How could you understand? You're not a girl. I was romantic, eager for love, swept off my feet by a glamorous foreigner. Paolo and I scarcely knew each other. We married in a whirlwind and then he died shortly afterwards.'

'And in between?' Domenico's voice pierced and wounded. Nicola looked at him angrily, on the point of tears, her eyes wide and wet.

'In between . . . what do you want me to say? That I discovered that my husband was a hot-headed gambler, that he loved to drive cars too fast and to flirt with every pretty girl he met, that he spent money as if it was water ...' The words spilled out hotly, flooding out of her in aching gasps. 'How do you think I felt when he was killed? Torn between a ghastly sort of relief and a terrible anguish of guilt and remembered love? I was in hell for months!'

They had entered the Farenze gates. The lions snarled down, paws upraised as though to strike her. She was sobbing wildly, her whole body shaking with grief and the complete breakdown of her long silence about Paolo.

Domenico braked. The car shot to a smooth halt beneath the trees. He turned in his seat, his hands reaching out for her.

'*Cara*,' he whispered huskily, 'I am sorry. So this is how it really was ...'

She pushed him back, trembling violently. 'Please ... I can't bear it ... I must go.'

Before he could stop her she had opened the door of the car, slipped out and begun to run away, into the cool depths of the formal garden. He, too, climbed out of the car, as if to follow her, then paused and stood, one hand on the warm bonnet, staring after her.

She passed out of sight behind a hedge. The grey eyes gazed blankly over the statues, the gravel paths, the ferny banks beneath the trees. Then Domenico climbed back into his car and drove on to the house, his lean face a cool mask.

CHAPTER TEN

LORENZO himself had promised to speak to Vanessa about staying on for a few more days in order to be at the Villa for the party given in her sister's honour.

Nicola went straight to her sister's room, when she had washed and changed after her weeping, and found Vanessa sitting on the bed contemplating a long evening dress of a heavenly blue shade, full-sleeved and low-necked, with great sweeping skirts which swished and murmured most satisfactorily with every movement.

'I gather,' Nicola said with amusement, 'that Lorenzo persuaded you to change your mind?'

'Mmmm ... Nicky, what do you think? This dress or the white one? This is gorgeous, but the white one does something for me.'

'I should wear this one,' Nicola said firmly. 'It's more romantic.'

'Do you think so?' Vanessa studied it, head to one side. 'I want to look positively stunning, Nicky. I want to make him sit up and take notice. I want to knock him for six. Do you think this is the right dress for all that?'

'Wear it and see,' came the answer.

'Oh, but I have just this one last chance. I can't afford a gamble—it must come off.' Vanessa's voice had a strange, dry desperation which wrung Nicola's heart. Her lovely sister had been tumbled off her pedestal with a vengeance!

'You won't have much competition,' she pointed out gently, but Vanessa merely sighed.

'You'll be there. Do you think I don't know he prefers you?'

Flushing, Nicola said, 'You're wrong, Van. Really —it may sound corny, but we're just good friends. There's never been anything more than that.'

Vanesa fixed her wide blue eyes on her. 'I can't believe it. He's spent such a lot of time with you—painting you hour after hour, alone with him in that ridiculous tower place ...'

'Leo means nothing to me, or I to him.'

Something about the certainty in Nicola's voice managed to get through. Vanessa looked at her sharply, probingly, and apparently believed her.

'Well, that's one family problem the less,' she said with rueful amusement.

Nicola was suddenly touched. 'You suspected that Leo and I were ... well, romantically entwined? Yet you didn't reproach me at all? You were very unselfish, Vanessa.'

'If he loved you what point was there in saying anything? Only after I realised you weren't in love with him, even though I still thought he liked you, only then could I bear to let you know how I felt.'

162

'How did you guess I didn't love him?' Nicola asked curiously.

Vanessa hesitated. 'I ... don't quite know how ...' She looked shyly at her sister. 'I saw you looking at Domenico—I'm sorry, I wasn't being vulgarly curious. It just dawned on me.'

Nicola laughed. 'We're a couple of lunatics, aren't we? Falling for men who ignore us! Perhaps we'd better both go home.'

That evening, after dinner, she and Lorenzo sat and wrote out the invitation envelopes and slid the stiff, silver-edged cards into them, firmly stamping them and putting them into a neat pile.

Leo strolled over to watch them. 'Am I invited to this extravaganza?'

'Of course. Only behave yourself.' Lorenzo gave him a long, stern look.

Bianca, sitting to one side with pale, angry features averted from them, stiffened even further as she heard these words, and Nicola felt an icy little chill as the black eyes darted sidelong in bitter hostility.

She had ceased to make little overtures to the other girl. Bianca merely rejected her coldly, contempt in every line of her face. She saw Nicola's wish to be friendly as a sign of weakness, and despised her. Bianca's Italian blood was productive of great pride and hauteur. She would rather have died than try to win over an enemy; jealousy and envy had corroded her mind. When Domenico came back into the room, having been to speak to someone on the telephone, Bianca tried to

163

draw him to her with an eager smile. He gave her a brief, faint smile in return, but came to sit beside Lorenzo to speak to him.

They discussed some business matter for a moment or two, then Domenico glanced, at length, at Nicola. During dinner he had avoided her. He had been almost silent, withdrawn, but now the grey eyes alighted on her face, stripping her emotions mercilessly.

She shrank from them, involuntarily, lowering her own eyes in self defence. Domenico's hard mouth compressed further. The grey eyes narrowed to mere flinty slits.

Leo, glancing from one to the other, was engrossed in amused speculation.

'I'm tired,' she said hastily, jumping up. 'Lorenzo, will you excuse me if I go up to bed now? I think I did too much walking in Florence today. I was on my feet all afternoon in the sunshine, and it's given me a slight headache.'

The old man frowned. 'I am sorry to hear that, *mia cara*. Have you some tablets to take? Shall we find you something? A cachet?'

'I have some tablets, thank you,' she said, smiling gratefully down at him.

Leo unexpectedly stood up, his carriage easy and lazy, and to her total astonishment kissed her lightly on her mouth. The black eyes danced as he grinned down at her astonished face.

'Goodnight, my dear Nicola,' he murmured softly. 'Sleep well.'

The silence in the room was profound. She could feel the eyes of everyone there fixed upon her. Lorenzo was startled, quizzical, a little annoyed with Leo. Domenico was grim, watchful. And Vanessa ... she dared not even look at her sister.

Stumbling to the door, Nicola felt dizzy and sick with the combined effect of her afternoon in the sun, and the shock of Leo's kiss. Leo, naturally, had been mischievous. The kiss had been a tease. But for whom?

She made her way to her bedroom and opened the door. While she was doing the cooking, Angelina had removed Paul to her room so that he should not disturb his mother when she was tired in the early morning. The room lay silent and empty in front of her. Nicola moved wearily towards the bed and switched on the lamp beside it.

Then she screamed. On the coverlet of her bed lay Paul's teddy bear. He had been disembowelled—his stuffing lay scattered on the bed. His head had been wrenched off and lay at the foot of the bed, the glass eyes staring sadly up at the ceiling.

Running footsteps sounded on the marble floors somewhere and Domenico burst into the room. 'Are you all right?' He raced across to her, caught her, his arm around her back, and looked at her searchingly. 'Why did you scream?'

Nicola was shaking, sickened not so much by the sight of the teddy bear as by the hatred behind the senseless act of destruction.

His eyes rose, saw the bed, narrowed as he took it all

165

in. 'My faith!' he breathed savagely. 'Who did this?'
Then his glance moved to the dressing-table. She saw
his face tighten yet further, and she, too, turned to look.

Across the mirror, written in scarlet lipstick, was the
one word *Morte* ... Death!

She could not stop the trembling of her body. Slump-
ing down on the edge of the bed, she whispered,
'Please, call Vanessa ... I can't sleep here tonight ...'

'No, no, of course.' He hesitated. 'Will you be all
right if I leave you?' But at that moment Vanessa and
Leo came into the room together.

'What was it? A rat?' Leo's tone was amused for a
moment, but he suddenly saw the remains of the teddy
bear, and the writing on the mirror, and his smile
faded. 'My God!'

The hostility between him and Domenico was evi-
dent as the other man let go of Nicola and turned to
face Leo. 'I suppose we do not need to look far to find
the perpetrator of this disgusting piece of work?'

Leo met his glare unsmilingly. 'Bianca? The girl is
sick, I think. If she did this ...'

'If?' Domenico's voice was harsh. 'Can you doubt it?
Who else would have done such a thing?'

Leo's face lengthened. 'What am I to do with her?
She must be so unhappy to do such things. I am at a
loss.' He looked at Nicola. '*Cara*, I am sorry—what can
I say to you? I am ashamed that my sister does these
things.'

'Why don't you send her back to your parents in

South America?' suggested Vanessa quietly. 'They are the right people to deal with the problem.'

Leo looked at her with dawning excitement. 'But of course—why didn't I think of it? That is what I shall do. She needs love and care and security.'

'You can't send her back,' Domenico said curtly.

Nicola looked at him in pain. He meant that he would look after Bianca, of course, that she must stay here at the Villa.

Nicola closed her eyes. She was so tired. If only they would all be quiet, let her sleep. She could almost sleep where she sat . . . yet not quite, for how could she bear this room now, with its echo of bitter hatred? The room was filled with dark memories, haunted by Bianca's unhappiness and desire to wound. The girl had come in here stealthily, taken a child's toy and destroyed it, deliberately and savagely. There was something terrifying in the destruction she had wreaked upon such an object. Nicola could not quite banish an unbidden thought—that, with a little more time, Bianca's sickness might bring her to worse deeds. Paul himself, helpless child though he was, might conceivably have been her final target.

She shuddered as the idea took hold in her mind. Paul! Her little baby. In such hideous danger!

An icy coldness seized her limbs. Bianca's mind was poisoned, she reminded herself. In a way what she had done had been a cry for help—wasn't that what the medical jargon usually said? There was much to be said for it, she told herself wearily. She had seen from the start that Bianca was unhappy. No healthy, normal mind had commited these acts.

Aloud she said, 'I'm sorry for her. Very sorry ...' She opened her eyes. The room was spinning round, in a strange fashion. Faces revolved, too—Vanessa's frowning, Leo, white and disturbed. And Domenico ... She looked at him in drowning regret, then Vanessa bent and said, 'Come on, honey. You can share my pad tonight.' Nicola began to cry then, at the kindness in her sister's voice.

She slept deeply that night, but it was a sleep disturbed by dreams. She found herself in the Villa garden, running down the alleys between the clipped green hedges, facing a vista of blind walls which always seem to recede before her. She could smell the scent of rain on the leaves, hear birds calling sweetly somewhere not too far off. But the silence of the garden held her as immovably as a shimmering spider's web holds a fly. Her brain was thudding with terror, her pulses beat dizzyingly. She knew she had to go on running, running. But why?

Then she saw Paul, standing on the top of one of the blind walls. He called, holding out his arms. She tried to answer, but her throat was parched and dumb.

Then Bianca came along the wall towards him, lips stretched in a soundless, terrifying smile. Nicola knew Bianca would push him, knew he would fall and be killed.

She screamed, then, again and again, and suddenly found herself on the wall in Paul's place. He had vanished. Bianca laughed and pushed her, hard, and she began to fall, slowly, her skirts spreading out like a parachute. Down and down she fell, with that strange, echoing slow motion which dreams often show us. Panic and fear made her stomach rise, and she closed her eyes against the relentless pull of gravity.

She opened them again, on a daylit bedroom, with the scent of coffee fragrant in her nostrils, and Vanessa seated, cross-legged, on the end of the bed, smiling at her.

'Welcome back to the land of the living. You slept like a log.'

'What time is it?' Nicola turned her head to look at the bedside table. The little jade glass clock showed the time as ten-fifteen. She was aghast. 'That late?' She moved hurriedly, to get out of bed, but Vanessa laid a compelling hand on her arm.

'Hang on a minute! You're to stay in bed until lunchtime!'

'Who said so?'

'Would you believe, Lorenzo?' Vanessa laughed. 'He was very upset about last night.'

'They didn't tell him about the bear? They shouldn't have done so! It might have alarmed him and brought on another stroke!'

'He can't be wrapped in cotton wool for the rest of his life,' Vanessa said. 'Anyway, Domenico didn't give

169

him any details, just said Bianca had broken something of yours and upset you. Lorenzo was up in arms at once.'

'Domenico wants her to stay here,' said Nicola flatly. 'You heard what he said last night. He'll find a way to protect her.'

'He's taking her to South America,' Vanessa said lightly.

Nicola sat up. 'He *what*?' She stared at her sister, wide-eyed and incredulous. 'Domenico is going all the way to South America with Bianca?'

Vanessa shrugged. 'Apparently he has business contacts with a firm over there and he decided to kill two birds with one stone—take Bianca home and do some business at the same time.'

'When are they going?'

Vanessa began to pour them both a cup of coffee, and pushed one cup over to Nicola's side of the tray. 'They've gone,' she said succinctly.

'What, already?' Nicola's hand shook slightly as she picked up her cup.

'Domenico doesn't hang about, does he?' Vanessa offered her a roll. 'Once he's made a decision—wham!' She whistled softly. 'He really is quite something— but marriage with him would be like living with a steamroller. Butter? Cherry jam?'

Nicola automatically took butter, dipped a spoon in the luscious thick black cherry jam and spread it on her roll. 'So Domenico won't be here for the party?'

'I doubt it!' Vanessa shot her a curious glance. 'Is it

serious with you, Nicky? I mean, are you trying to fight it off? I've had symptoms of love before now, but I've treated them like the onset of a cold, and dosed myself against them.'

Nicola laughed huskily. 'What do you take? I may need the advice.'

'I make myself notice all his bad points. I mentally make fun of him and laugh myself out of it.' Vanessa was half serious.

'Did you do that with Leo?' asked Nicola.

Vanessa sighed. 'Frequently. It didn't work for once, so I just gave up the unequal struggle.'

'Was that painful?'

Vanessa gave her a grin. 'Honey, it was a relief!'

'A relief?' Nicola was amused. She sipped her coffee and felt the warmth spreading through her chilled body, untangling the conflicts of the long night.

Vanessa ran her fingers through her blonde curls. 'It is a strain, fighting off love. One gets tired of the struggle. I think maybe I was ready to meet Leo—success is wearing, and I knew I couldn't stay at the top of the modelling tree for much longer. I'm not a young girl any more. I've had a fantastic career, but even that's lost its original excitement.'

'Bored with your career, Van?' Nicola smiled away the sting of her mockery. 'I can't believe it!'

'Maybe I'm not as tough and opportunistic as I thought I was,' said Vanessa. 'When I came out here with you it was to further my chances of snatching Domenico—you knew that. I would have sold you down the river then, Nicky. I wanted to grab him while I had the chance. Then one look at Leo and my world went topsy-turvy.' She grimaced. 'And, in a crazy sort of way, I was thrilled. It was twice as exciting as my success as a model. I felt dizzy and elated at one and the same time. So I let go all my old ideas and just ...' she spread her hands in an expressive gesture, 'just fell all the way down.'

Nicola touched her hand gently. 'I wish he would feel the same way, Vanessa. Maybe if you stayed ...'

Vanessa shook her head. 'I'll stay until the party, then I'm going. I'm not sorry I ever met him, Nicky—I'm glad, even if he never looks at me. It was worth it.'

'I'll miss you,' said Nicola. 'It was fun sharing a flat with you and Bess.'

'You'll stay here at the Villa, of course,' her sister replied casually. 'I'm glad you've seen sense over that. Paul's happy here, much happier than he was in that cramped little flat in London. He has so many people around him; Angelina, Lorenzo, the Italian kids that come to play with him twice a week. He has room and sunshine—what more could he want?'

Nicola sighed. 'I shall be homesick now and then. And there's the problem of Domenico.'

'Domenico?'

'It will be unbearable, living here in the same house, knowing he is indifferent to me.'

Vanessa nodded sympathetically. 'Maybe it will be all for the best if he marries Bianca and stays over in South America!'

Nicola was silent, her body shocked into immobility. Then, in a dry voice, she asked, 'Is that what you think he'll do? Did he actually say so?'

Shrugging, Vanessa said, 'No, he didn't actually say so, but it looks pretty obvious, doesn't it, Nicky? Why else would he go all that way just for her? Why would he protect her as he has? He must be serious about her, and, let's face it, Bianca may be a little screwy, but she's a ravishingly lovely girl. Just the dark-eyed beauty for an Italian like Domenico.'

Nicola walked stiffly over to her wardrobe and began to search for something to wear. Her fingers moved through the clothes, but her mind was abstracted. Vanessa was right, of course—Domenico must be in love with Bianca. Perhaps he would never come back to the Villa Farenze, and she might never see him again. It would, in a way, be the kindest thing, for her own sake, this sudden, unexpected parting, and although it hurt now she would recover quicker, as one does from one swift, sure cut from the knife of a surgeon. She told herself so, calmly and soberly, but it made no difference. It hurt intolerably just the same.

CHAPTER ELEVEN

WITH Domenico out of the way, and Nicola released from her self-imposed duties in the kitchen, Leo insisted that she spend most of the daylight hours in his studio posing for him. He was in a hurry to finish his portrait of her so that he could present it to Lorenzo at the party. She brought Paul with her several times so that Leo could draw him, but Paul would not sit still long enough for any detailed pose to be possible. He wriggled and shouted to get down, and was very interested in the paints and filthy pieces of paint-daubed cloth which Leo left strewn around the room.

'He's like an eel,' Leo said discontentedly, watching the little boy squeezing an empty tube and crowing with delight as a tiny squirm of white paint oozed out. 'Put that down, you imp of hell! You'll get dirty and then Angelina will nag me until my ears drop off.'

Paul laughed and toddled off to peer over the windowsill at the earth far below. Catching him hurriedly around his small waist, Nicola looked down too, her head circling dizzily for a moment. Green and leafy, the world seemed to revolve far below. She saw Vanessa strolling along an alley in the garden, her full skirt blowing back from her slender legs. Leo joined them and Nicola, glancing up, caught an odd expression on his handsome face.

Her suspicions arose, but she quelled them firmly. She was rather too eager to believe that Leo had some hidden interest in Vanessa—she refused to allow herself to be too hopeful.

'Your beautiful sister seems to be at a loose end since Domenico went off to South America,' he drawled over her head.

Carefully staring out of the window, she said casually, 'Oh, Vanessa wasn't ever really interested in Domenico.'

'No?' He sounded doubtful. 'She gave a good imitation.'

'Vanessa has always had a lot of admirers,' Nicola said. 'She moves in that sort of world—models attract men like flies, but it doesn't mean anything very much.'

'Just routine? A flirtation and then goodbye—*ciao*!' He made a practised gesture, halfway between a shrug and a wave. 'I somehow don't think Domenico knew that!'

Slowly, Nicola asked, 'You think he was more serious than that?'

'She's very beautiful.' Leo's voice was husky. Nicola hazarded another quick glance upwards. He was staring down at Vanessa, his face unguarded briefly. Nicola drew in her breath in surprise and embarrassment at what she saw in that dark face now. Leo looked down hastily, met her eyes and dark angry colour rose in his cheeks. The black eyes flashed.

175

'I'm sorry, Leo,' she stammered. 'I ... didn't know ... you gave me no inkling that you felt like ...' Her voice died away as she realised the sheer absurdity of trying to apologise. What could she say? She had seen something he had tried to keep hidden—once more, as when she had seen his portfolio of sketches of Vanessa and misinterpreted them as hatred. They had been the product of angry emotion, but it had been love, not hate, that dictated them.

Once she would have blithely seen this as a happy ending. Vanessa was in love with Leo. Now, it seemed, Leo loved her, too. Nicola sighed. Maturity brought new problems. Her own marriage to Paolo had taught her that love is not always enough. She had loved Paolo, but her memories of him were tainted by her realisation that he was not, in fact, the man she had believed him to be when she married him. Side by side with her love an angry dislike had grown—a dislike of what he did rather than of Paolo himself. She had not ceased to love, but she had ceased to be happy with him.

Leo, she saw, disliked some of Vanessa's characteristics. Unlike herself, Leo had seen these faults from the start. He was attracted to Vanessa, yet saw her clearly. Could any marriage prosper with such a foundation? Could Vanessa be happy with a man who brought to their relationship the clear-eyed perception which Leo had shown in those sketches of her?

Leo passed one hand over his face. 'You should have taken up art,' he said hoarsely. 'You have extra-sensory

176

perception, I think—or X-ray eyes! I hope you'll forget it, now, though. No heart-to-heart chats with big sister?' His eyes flashed to her face, held her own gaze soberly. 'Promise? This is an official secret!'

She hesitated. He did not, of course, know how Vanessa felt. But would he change his mind, even if he did? She did not know him well enough. He had read Vanessa as an ambitious, hard-headed woman capable of callous and cruel determination in the pursuit of her ends—the sketches had made that brutally plain. If Leo knew that Vanessa loved him, would he alter his opinion of her?

Leo shook her, frowning. 'Did you hear me? Promise not to say a word to your sister.'

'I promise,' she said reluctantly, then dived to intercept Paul, who had crawled into an interesting tunnel made by some paintings leaning against a wall. She pulled him out, hoisted him into her arms and said goodbye to Leo.

'We must go to lunch.'

He nodded. 'I think I've got as much as I need. He is the world's worst model. I'll concentrate on the background now. I've only got one more day to finish off.'

'Do you want me to come over again?' she asked.

He shook his head. 'No, I don't think so, thank you. Your face is finished.'

'Can I see?' She had not yet set eyes on the picture and was longing to see it.

'No,' he said firmly. 'You can wait, like everyone else. You'll see it in good time.'

177

Signora Farenze was in the courtyard when Paul and Nicola came back into the house. A shaft of sunlight fell short of her chair, leaving her in shadow. She wore her usual black dress and was reading a newspaper, her spectacles on the end of her nose. She peered over them and smiled.

'Paul! How are you today?'

'Hungry,' he said, bouncing over to her. 'I could eat a horse!'

'So hungry? How terrible! Fortunate that here comes Angelina to rescue you from this starvation ...'

Angelina came soft-footed and seized him, shrieking with delight. She smiled at Nicola and bade her good-day with an affection which, on that first day of their arrival, Nicola could not have predicted. How much all their attitudes had changed, she thought, watching as her son was carried off, chattering excitedly while Angelina listened in amused fascination.

Signora Farenze looked up at her shrewdly. 'You are thoughtful today, *mia cara*?'

'The party has made me excited, I suppose,' said Nicola, a little evasively.

The old blue eyes narrowed. 'The party? And Leo's portrait of you, eh?'

Blankly, Nicola said, 'The portrait? Oh, that ... yes, I suppose that, too.'

Watching her carefully, Signora Farenze said, 'I hope you were not too angry with little Bianca? She has had a disturbed childhood—so often away from her parents during her early years, and never really feeling

178

she belonged anywhere, even here at the Villa. I do not think her actions were truly personal.'

'I think she loved Paolo,' Nicola said firmly. 'That is how I read the situation. She was in love with him, and hated me for marrying him. But how can we ever really understand the motives of other people? Even when they tell us why they did things, it may not be the real truth. People often quite unconsciously rationalise their motives even to themselves.'

Signora Farenze inclined her head slowly in assent. 'You are right. Bianca's motives were probably more complex than we know. But you do not feel that what she did could influence your feelings for her brother?'

Nicola flushed. 'For Leo? No. Why should it? I like Leo. He's far more serious than he appears on the surface, and I'm sorry for him in some ways. Bianca and he were never very close, I gather.'

'No, they did not live together in childhood. Leo was sent to boarding-school and then to art college. He has only really known Bianca well since she came to live in the watch-tower. She came to the Villa, too, with the idea of living there with him, but Lorenzo insisted that she lived in the house, here. It was more suitable.'

'Lorenzo has been good to them,' Nicola commented.

Signora Farenze shrugged. 'They are of the family!' She studied Nicola closely. 'I will be frank with you, *mia cara*. Are you in love with Leo?'

Nicola shook her head. 'No.'

179

There was a little silence, then the old woman sighed gently. 'I am glad—so glad, *cara*.'

Nicola laughed. 'Why?'

Signora Farenze smiled. 'He is not the right man for you.'

On the evening of the party, Nicola got dressed carefully and went down to inspect the salons which had been prepared for the guests.

A cold buffet had been laid out on the damask-draped tables in the dining-room. Silverware, glass and immaculate white napkins added the finishing touches to a beautifully laid meal. The piles of plates at each end of the tables, the elegantly arranged flowers, had all been seen to earlier. Bowls of salad, cut slices of bread and piles of freshly baked rolls stood along the back of the table.

Arrayed in front of these were salmon and egg mousses, caviar, cold rice with prawns and vegetables, paper-thin slices of Parma ham with melon, cold legs of chicken, cheese and pickles, and many other party dishes.

Nicola wiped a finger over a glass to check the cleanliness, nodded in satisfaction and wiped the glass again with a napkin. She put one last touch to a flower arrangement, then stood back. She could find no fault with it.

'Where is the champagne?' Lorenzo came up behind her and made her jump.

'In the kitchen, being kept at the right temperature.'

She looked at him inquiringly. 'Well? Are you pleased?'

He looked round the room. 'Sure. It looks fine.' He spoke in English, jokingly, then with a grin of relief reverted to his own tongue. 'You look very beautiful, *mia cara*. I shall be very proud of you tonight.'

'She looks like a firebird,' said Leo, coming in from the courtyard through the open window.

Eagerly, the old wrinkled face turned to him. 'The portrait? Where is it?'

'It isn't quite finished, you know,' Leo said warningly. 'It isn't framed, and I have a lot of last touches to make.'

'But I can see it? You promised we could put it on show tonight to the guests.' Lorenzo looked disappointed.

Leo shrugged. 'Just as you like. I brought it over—but if anybody lays a finger on it I won't be responsible. The paint isn't quite dry yet. It takes days to dry off properly.'

'Let me see it,' Lorenzo implored.

Leo went back into the courtyard and came back at once, wheeling an easel on a small metal frame supported by two wheels, rather like the base of a shopping bag on wheels. He rested this in one corner and delicately whisked off the cover.

The others walked forward slowly. The portrait had a formal background—for a moment Nicola could not quite decide what it was, but then she suddenly realised that it was the garden of the Villa; the alleys and

181

hedges, the green cypress and box trees, the fountain in the centre, spraying silver droplets of liquid around the mossy paths. In the foreground she sat, Paul on her lap, her face faintly darkened by the shadow of a cypress. She was smiling at the child, a gentle, mysterious smile which made her face unfamiliar to her. She felt quite peculiar as she stared at this representation of herself. It looked like her, yet not like her.

Paul, however, was distinctly himself. His fine-featured face, delicate and golden-skinned, was alive with laughter and mischief. He was leaping up to kiss her, his plump hand on her throat. The dark hair, dark eyes and Roman nose were all there, softened in baby-hood, yet oddly reminiscent of the features of the old man who stood in front of the painting lost in silence.

Leo was pale. He shifted nervously, watching them like a hawk. 'Well?' His voice was hoarse.

Lorenzo slowly turned to look at him. Without one word he opened his arms wide and Leo instinctively moved into the embrace. Lorenzo kissed him on both cheeks, patting his shoulders. There were tears in his dark eyes.

Nicola watched sympathetically, close to tears herself. Leo, freed from his uncle's embrace, turned to look at her, and she smiled at him.

'You've taken my breath away, Leo,' she said. 'The painting is so beautiful!'

Leo's mercurial spirits soared. He seized her, kissed her warmly on the lips, his hands holding her shoulders lightly. Vanessa, walking into the room at that exact moment, stood stock still and stared with wide-stretched eyes in a pale face.

Leo looked up as he released Nicola and saw her. On the new flood of his delight, he grinned wickedly. 'To-night is a festival of love,' he said lightly. 'No one escapes without paying a forfeit.' He reached out to take Vanessa's arm, pulled her close and bent to kiss her.

Angrily, she pulled away, her free hand pushing at his chest. Leo was aroused. His dark face reddened, then he dragged her forcibly into his arms and kissed her hard, his bent head showing a red stain of rage where the black hair ended.

Lorenzo looked shocked, then amused. Silently he tiptoed out, winking at Nicola as she followed him.

Vanessa, taken off guard, melted into Leo's arms, her own hands curving up to stroke the curly hair. There was a long silence in the salon, then Leo abruptly pushed her away from him, looked down at her with narrowed eyes and strode out of the room.

Vanessa remained, her hand at her lips, trembling.

The guests were met at the entrance to the main salon by Lorenzo, erect and smiling in his black dinner jacket, with Nicola at his side in a long dress of white chiffon, tied at the waist by a sash of purple, and with a matching purple edging to the layered sleeves, which fell in widening cascades to her wrist. Her hair was looped through a golden ring and fell in a sleek curve to her shoulders.

A small cluster of musicians played a mixture of popular music and popular classics in the courtyard. The door into the garden was left wide open so that those guests who chose to stroll there, in the light of some coloured fairy lights strung from trees and bushes, could enjoy the distant lilt of the music.

Nicola began to have a sense of complete unreality after a time. She shook hands with Farenze after Farenze; Antonio, Pietro, Vicenzo— the names clicked in her head while the faces came and went, dark, smiling, curious faces which all bore a strange resemblance one to the other. They complimented her on her son, admired the portrait, which Lorenzo had had placed prominently nearby, stared and visibly noted Lorenzo's affection for her.

Vanessa stood nearby, with Leo and Signora Farenze, distinctly the second string of the welcoming party. Leo was very distinguished in black evening clothes, pale and oddly withdrawn on such a gay occasion. Now and then he and Vanessa exchanged glances. Their eyes met and rapidly drew away again. Vanessa was trembling slightly, her blue eyes very bright and feverlit. She had not spoken to him since their kiss. It lay between them, though, as a crater marks the site of an explosion, and they each guardedly walked around it.

When most of the guests had arrived, Lorenzo and Nicola began to circulate, talking at more leisure to those whom Lorenzo was particularly eager for her to meet.

184

She smiled and answered polite questions with polite answers, and wondered with sombre resignation where Domenico was now—in what tropical heat did he sit, with Bianca, sipping wine and watching the distant stars of the South American sky? Half of her nature seemed dead. She had to keep up appearances, for Lorenzo's sake, but it cost her a great deal to smile and pretend gaiety.

Once or twice she glanced around to watch her sister, looking fragile and romantic in her drifting blue dress, the centre of an admiring crowd. Leo was somewhere on the periphery, watching Vanessa too, with his dark eyes narrowed.

Nicola wondered if, after all, there was hope for them. If they truly loved each other they might overcome all the barriers that nationality and personality could erect between them. Like a bulldozer love can smash all obstacles, she thought sadly.

A plump dark matron in vivid red silk, still carrying the traces of a once remarkable beauty, spoke to her, and she turned back to listen, smiling courteously. Lorenzo, under cover of his hand, winked at her, and her eyes flicked back an amused gratitude for his kindness and understanding.

Half an hour later Lorenzo held up his hand for silence, standing on a chair so that all the guests could see him. 'A cold buffet is laid out in the dining-room, and I hope you will all enjoy the food, but first, my friends and members of the Farenze family—I have a

185

small ceremony to perform!' He slid a hand inside his dinner jacket, brought out a flat case.

'There is a tradition in the family—you will all have heard about it. The bride of the eldest son wears the Farenze emeralds.' He looked down at Nicola's suddenly astonished face and smiled. 'Well,' he went on, 'Nicola is my son's widow and she has never formally taken possession of what is hers by right. She knows, as you all must know, that I did not welcome her marriage. I want you all to hear me tell her now that I bitterly regret that stupidity. She is more than I deserved—she is the most enchanting bride any Farenze has ever brought into our family, and I am honoured and proud to give her these emeralds.' He bent and handed her the case with a flourish.

She automatically took it, stared at it, then stammered something incoherent.

Lorenzo laughed. 'You see how modest she is, my English daughter-in-law? She says she does not want them, the emeralds which the Farenzes have treasured for centuries! Men have died for them, yet Nicola does not want them!'

The guests laughed politely, but there were curious, hungry gleams in the eyes of some of them as they stared at the flat blue case.

Lorenzo took it back from her, eyeing her bent head with some tenderness. But Nicola was too embarrassed by the public interest in all this to do anything but stare at the floor.

Fumblingly, the old man opened the case and took

out the necklace. It hung from his two hands, flashing like green flames as it moved through the air. He bent and slid it around her throat, and she jumped as the cold stones came to rest against her warm skin. The other guests gave a long sigh of pleasure, staring at the beautiful things, but Nicola felt unbearably trapped.

She looked up, desperately, then her heart gave a leap of joy and pain, for there, at the salon door, stood Domenico.

His grey eyes met hers with cool evaluation, and un-knowingly she sent him a silent plea for help. He came towards her, through the crowd, and Lorenzo beamed down at him.

'Domenico!' Pleasure and affection lit the wrinkled old face. 'You are back! How is Bianca now?'

'She is safely with her parents,' Domenico said quietly. 'But now, Lorenzo, you have monopolised Nicola long enough. I think I may claim the pleasure of taking her in to supper.'

Lorenzo's shrewd eyes slid from one to the other, then a cunning smile crept over his face. 'Of course, of course,' he said enthusiastically.

Domenico crooked his arm and bowed. Shyly, Nicola slid her hand through his arm. The crowd parted, and curious, knowing eyes followed their progress into the courtyard.

The shadows swallowed them. The musicians, play-ing with hot, perspiring faces, watched them walk through the garden gate into the starry night.

Nicola's legs trembled beneath her as she walked.

She swallowed. What did this return mean? Was Domenico, then, not intending to marry Bianca after all? Or had it merely been postponed while she recovered her health?

She glanced up at him. His profile was cool and unreadable as ever.

Huskily she said, 'I wasn't expecting you back tonight. You were not in South America long.'

'I was longer than I could have wished,' he said. 'It seemed an eternity.'

She wondered what that meant. A strange, hesitant sort of happiness was beginning to spread through her veins. She was afraid to believe what she saw in his eyes.

'My mother tells me she is certain you do not love Leo,' he said abruptly, and this very roughness was excitingly hopeful, for Domenico was not usually so lacking in poise.

'I told you that myself,' she said softly.

He stood still, turning towards her. The warm dark sky spread overhead. There was a gentle sound of cicadas, and the breeze stirred in the cypresses.

Nicola looked up into Domenico's dark face with wide, incredulous eyes. Could she be mad, or was that a growing hunger she saw in his face?

His hands gripped her elbows. Thickly, he murmured, 'You know I have been jealous of Leo, jealous of Paolo, of every man who ever looked at you? I think I loved you even before I met you, from the first time I saw that photograph of you which Paolo sent me so long ago ...' He released her and took out his wallet, brought out of it a small snapshot, a little crumpled and yellowing. Nicola stared in disbelief, then laughed.

Her own face, years younger in time and experience, looked up at her.

'You kept it?'

He grimaced wryly. 'All these years! Yes. I even cut Paolo off—after I had met you in England. Because I knew then, *mia cara, mia carissima ...*'

She was still incredulous. 'You were very unkind to me then, Domenico.'

'I was sick with hunger,' he said thickly. 'Nicola, could you ever ...' His voice faded, but his eyes spoke for him.

She laughed, on a caught breath. 'Nico!'

Then she was in his arms and sky, stars, warm breathing garden vanished in a whirl of sparks more fiery and more dramatic than the Farenze emeralds. She clung, kissing him back with all the love and hunger of long starvation, and he held her so that she thought her bones must crack under the impact.

When at last she raised her head the world spun in a dizzying circle, but she merely laughed, and framed his lean face in the cup of her two hands.

'I love you, Domenico Farenze, more than I loved Paolo, more than I thought possible for any woman to love any man. If that will not satisfy you, I'm sorry— it's the best I can do today,' and she laughed up at him. 'Tomorrow I hope I'll do better!'

189

By popular demand...

24 original novels from this series—by 7 of the world's greatest romance authors.

These back issues have been out of print for some time. So don't miss out; order your copies now!

Harlequin Reader Service
ORDER FORM